A Riot in Murphy's Pub

Irene Melaugh

A Riot in Murphy's Pub

Pegasus

PEGASUS PAPERBACK

© Copyright 2024
Irene Melaugh

The right of Irene Melaugh to be identified as author of
this work has been asserted by her in accordance with the
Copyright, Designs and Patents Act 1988.

A CIP catalogue record for this title is
available from the British Library.

ISBN 978 1 80468 039 1

This is a work of fiction. Names, characters, businesses, places, events and
incidents are either the product of the author's imagination or used in a
fictitious manner. Any resemblance to actual persons, living or dead, or actual
events is purely coincidental.

Pegasus is an imprint of
Pegasus Elliot Mackenzie Publishers Ltd.
www.pegasuspublishers.com

First Published in 2024

Pegasus
Sheraton House Castle Park
Cambridge England

Printed & Bound in Great Britain

In memory of Jilly Angell, my friend.

Acknowledgements

To my four children, for their love and support.
To Margie and Dolores, my lifelong friends.
To Elaine, for suggesting I write the book.

Chapter One

If Liam McBride had known the events that would unfold in the next forty-eight hours, he would never have set foot in Murphy's Pub that day. Monday started the same as any other. He got up, took a shower, dressed and went to work, expecting nothing but the usual boredom. A well-built man in his early thirties with ice-blue eyes, Liam looked more like a body builder than a barman. He had developed some extra muscles thanks to lifting heavy beer kegs, not to mention removing belligerent drunks from the premises on a Saturday night.

Hung-over from too much whiskey the previous night, he walked home and left his car parked across the street from Murphy's Pub. He sort of fell into the job. As a regular in the pub, he sometimes volunteered to pull a few pints behind the bar on the busier nights. He found he was as good at pulling pints as he was at drinking them. After a few years, the owner wanted to retire so Liam was offered first refusal on renting the pub. He accepted and he was still pulling pints and busting balls every Saturday night for the past ten years. There was nothing else to do in the village for entertainment but drink. The nearest cinema was twenty miles away in Derry. On rare occasions, a carload of locals would go only if the current movie involved any kind of controversy. The last time this happened was when 'In The Name Of The Father' was showing. After the movie, they all came back to Murphy's Pub and had a rowdy discussion about the injustice that was done to the six men, especially Giuseppe Conlon. Although everyone was on the same side, it still managed to end in a punch-up. Beating the shit out of each other was the only form of recreation and enjoyment the locals had.

Tullamoragh was the village where Liam was born and bred. He never imagined he would still be living there at his age. As a teenager, he had planned to travel and see as much of the world as he could. But circumstances and lack of money got in the way. Nestled in a corner of County Derry, Tullamorgh straddles the border with Donegal and is surrounded on all sides by luscious green fields that roll out like a multi-coloured patchwork quilt, all the way to the foothills of the Donegal Mountains two miles in the distance. As a rule, nothing much happens in Tullamoragh. The days come and go, and the weeks and the years. And so, time passes by with nothing much to mark one day as being different to the next. The biggest event ever to happen in the village was the kidnapping of Ned, a much-loved member of Donal O'Casey's family. The ransom note was left at Donal's front door demanding two hundred-and-fifty pounds for the victim's safe return. But the mayor, one Brendon Bowyer McBride, let it be known that his village did not do business with Kidnappers or terrorists. The next day, Ned the donkey was found safe and well, tied to the gates of the Catholic chapel.

Six hundred-and-forty- seven and one-half souls live in the Tullamoragh. Donal O'Casey's wife was pregnant again with her twenty- first child, the first twenty being girls. Donal had his fingers crossed again that, this time, it would be a son, an heir to take over the running of his small dairy farm when he is too old to work it anymore His wife has informed him that this was her last pregnancy so, if it was another girl, he can stop crossing his fingers and start crossing his legs.

The village has a small Protestant church, consisting of an altar and twenty-four pews. It was built in eighteen-ninety. Situated half-way up Lowery's Hill, it can be seen by everyone in the village. Not to be outdone, however, one year later, the Catholics built a larger church. It has an altar and thirty pews. Sitting proudly at the very top of Lowery's Hill, it signifies to all that Catholics are closer to heaven than Protestants.

The majority of the village's population are farmers. However, there is the recent opening of a small makeshift clothing factory that produces high-visibility garments. This venture caused the employment rate in the village to shoot through the roof, adding ten women and one man to the work force. Mayor McBride was responsible for bringing the venture to the village and he never lets anyone forget it. Tullamoragh has two grocery shops, each in great competition with the other. By far the most popular of the two is Joe's Wee Shop. It first opened in eighteen eighty-eight by the Rafferty family and it has never changed hands or its name in all that time. Every Joe in a long line of Joes has inherited Joe's Wee shop. The locals would tell you that every firstborn son was called Joe because the family was too tight to buy a new sign. The present owner, Joe, of course, has never married. A sight for sore eyes, he stands at five-feet-one-inch. He is totally bald with bulging frog-like eyes and a belly so big that, if he ever got tired of walking down the hill, he could lay on his belly and roll down to his shop. He still lives with his ninety-two-year-old mother. Over-protective and over-bearing, Mrs Rafferty had made it her business to see off the one female who had designs on Joe. And his shop. Every Saturday night, she accompanies her son to Murphy's Pub where she has a Sandy Man Port. And, if the Moon is in the right position to Mars, she might allow Joe to have two whole beers.

It's Saturday, market day in Tullamoragh. The day when farmers come to buy and sell livestock. A time to find out what nearly happened in the village since last Saturday. The twice-a-day bus pulled up and Liam jumped off just in time to be caught in a heavy downpour. He crossed the street, zig-zagging between a herd of cows and a forlorn-looking flock of drenched sheep. It was a short distance from the bus stop to the car park, where the many pot holes had now turned into swimming pools. He manoeuvred his way between the puddles, breathing a sigh of relief when he saw his car still standing. It was not much but it was all he owned in the world. He unlocked the driver's door and reached in to retrieve his ledger. And that's when he saw it. 'Shit!' He pulled the parking ticket from the wiper and shoved it into his pocket.

Joe had been watching the unfolding drama from the window of his shop across the street. Liam put the ledger under his arm and walked towards the shop.

'Do you never learn, man! You know from nine a.m. you need to buy a ticket.' Joe already had a twenty pack of cigarettes in his hand.

'Traffic wardens! They should all be bloody shot at birth.' Liam paid Joe, opened the packet and lit up.

Joe asked, 'Any craic?'

'Apart from the usual Friday night cracked skulls? Nothing!' He walked out of the shop to Murphy's Pub next door, something he had done every day for the past ten years. He opened the front door with his key and, at the same time, gave it a hefty kick. The door needed to be fixed. He'd get round to it one of these years. When he entered the bar, the smell of stale alcohol and illegal cigarette smoke made his eyes water. He looked around at the ramshackle bar and muttered, 'Another day in paradise!' He took off his wet coat, threw it on a stool and began to clear away dirty glasses from the equally dirty tables. A loud bang from the store room halted him in his tracks. Very quietly, he put the glasses down and grabbed a Hurley bat from behind the bar. He kicked the storeroom door open and rushed in with the Hurley bat held high above his head in both hands. Soupy lay face down on the floor between two beer kegs.

'Jesus, Soupy, I could have knocked your head off!'

Still face down but recognising Liam's voice, he managed to speak, ''Tis yourself, Liam? Didn't I think you were a burglar up to no good?'

'God give me patience!' He reached down and pulled Soupy to his feet, who stood swaying in a circular motion.

'Tell me now, what day is it?' A big toothless grin managed to deepen the crevices in his weather-beaten face even more.

'Out!' Liam grabbed him by his arm, ran him through the pub to the front door and pushed him out. 'And don't come back!'

'That man is going to give himself a hernia.' Soupy eyed a cigarette butt on the ground at his feet and bent down to retrieve it, but he staggered, falling backwards. He lay there for a few seconds as he tried to get his bearings. When his head stopped spinning, he picked up the butt, stuck it in his mouth and staggered down the street.

Liam had finished tidying up and was sitting behind the bar reading the paper, when Jerry O'Malley, the land lord, came in whistling.

'Hiya, Liam!' He sat on a bar stool.

'Jerry? This is a surprise.' Liam poured a glass of whiskey and slid it in front of him. 'Is anything wrong?' The only time Jerry ever came into the pub was on a Sunday morning to collect the rent.

'Well, there is and there isn't,' Jerry replied. 'You could say I have good news and bad news.' He swallowed the whiskey in one go and banged the empty glass down on the bar. 'I've been made an offer for the pub and I'm going to take it.'

'You're selling the pub? This is a bit sudden. Can I ask who's buying it?'

'No one you'd know. It's a Belfast group. They're offering me fifty thousand.'

'Fifty thousand!' Liam looked around the ramshackle room, with its faded wallpaper, torn seats and tables that were on their last legs, literally. 'Have they seen this place?'

'They aren't interested in what it looks like. They are only interested in the location. They are planning on building a boutique hotel. Can you believe it! The only guests they'll have at their hotel will be the field mice.'

Liam took a deep breath. 'Right. When is this going to happen?'

'It'll be a couple of months until the paperwork can be drawn up.' Jerry stood up. 'Well, that's that then.' When he reached the door he stopped and, almost as an afterthought, said, 'Of course, I would rather sell to you. So, if you can get your hands on fifty big ones?' He gave Liam a salute. 'Good luck now.' And he was gone.

'Jesus!' Liam poured himself a stiff whiskey and threw it back.

Chapter Two

It was closing time and Murphy's Pub was empty except for the usual stragglers. Liam wanted to get home. He'd had a headache all day, thanks to Jerry O'Malley.

Higs asks, 'I'll have another wee whiskey, if you please, Liam.'

'Last orders was half an hour ago.' Liam pulled the empty glass from Higs's hand.

'Right.' Bosco got down from the stool. 'I'll see you later, then. Come on, Soupy, I'll help you to stagger home.'

'Hey, Soupy,' Liam called. 'Where is the bookie slip?' But Soupy had left the building. ''Night, boys,' Higs shouted. 'See you tomorrow night, same time, same place.'

'I don't know why we waste our money doing accumulators. We never win.' Liam threw the newspaper in the bin. Higs was holding onto the bar for support.

'Come on now, Higs, it's bedtime.'

'Have you seen what's in my bed?'

Liam pulled on his coat. 'Well, you married her.'

'Aye, God help me, I did. What time is it?'

'It's one o'clock.'

'I'm in bother. I told her I'd be home at ten p.m.' Higs had a thought. 'I was just thinking, maybe I could sleep at yours?'

'Not a hope in hell! I'm not getting entangled in your marital problems. Come on, I have to get home to my dog.'

'I'll swap you your bitch for mine.'

Higs spent the next five minutes wrestling with the sleeves of his jacket. He eventually managed to get it on. Liam locked up the pub and tried to ignore Higs, who was leaning against the outside wall of the pub for support.

'Could you point me in the direction of that place?'

'What place is that?' Liam put the keys in his pocket.

'That place I laughingly call home.'

'Go to your left.'

'Right you are.' Higs started to walk but his legs wobbled and he fell to the ground. Exasperated, Liam pulled him back to his feet.

'Wait here. I'll give you a lift.'

'Good man, yourself.' Higs sat on the windowsill and waited.

Liam drove the car to the edge of the path, leant across, opened the passenger door and Higs fell in. The car drove off. Ten minutes later, they arrived at their destination. Liam elbowed the heavily-snoring Higs in the ribs.

'Wake up. You're home.'

'What? So soon?'

The front door of his house opened and the ample frame of his wife, Lila, appeared. She stood there, arms folded, glaring at her husband.

'Ah, there she is the love of my life,' he whispered to Liam. 'Did you know Martin McGuinness was terrified of that face? I suppose I better get out of the car then?'

'That would be a definite yes!' Liam reached across, opened the passenger door and Higs promptly fell out. He was spread-eagled on the ground.

'It's all right now. I'm all right! It's just a case of minor brain damage.'

Liam watched as Higs tried to squeeze past his wife's rigid body, getting stuck between the door frame and Lila's enormous breasts. There was a tussle that lasted thirty seconds, until he finally broke free and fell head-first into the hall. The front door shut with a bang and Liam made a quick getaway.

Higs managed to get to his feet. 'Well, now, Mrs Hegarty, how are you on this fine Friday night?'

'Its the early hours of Sunday morning!' she said through clenched teeth.

'Is it, indeed? Where does the time go?'

Lila was taller than her husband by a good head and shoulders. He tried to straighten himself up to his full height but he still only reached her chest. She looked down at him with a thunderous look on her face. Her breasts were so close they threatened to attack him again.

'I think I'll go to bed,' under his breath. 'Where, I fear, you will follow.' He started to climb the stairs, swaying precariously on the edge of each one. His wife watched him for a few seconds before reaching under the hall table and picking up a hatchet. She followed her husband slowly up the stairs.

It was Sunday morning and ten o'clock mass has just ended. Madge and Josie came out of the chapel and walked towards the gate where Madge took up sentinel duty to see who had not been at mass. The two women had been friends for a lifetime, through many trials and tribulations. The main tribulation being Josie's marriage to the village layabout, Sore Hole McSwine. Sore Hole was a reference to the time when, as a youth, he was caught running away from a riot and the British army riddled his arse with bullets. It was the making of him. He was able to claim every benefit in the book for his injuries. Apparently, he had a missing tail bone and so he was never able to sit down again. From that day onward, Sole Hole always lay down, no matter where he was. Madge never approved of him. She didn't think he was good enough for Josie, and she didn't think it was fair of Josie to get married when she wasn't. Anyway, Sore Hole's injuries finally caught up with him. On the day of their wedding, Josie and he were on a small rowing boat crossing from the main land over to Inch Island for their honeymoon night. He was at the bottom of the boat, flat on his back as usual, when it suddenly capsized. Josie was able to hold onto the boat and be rescued, but Sore Hole went straight down to the bottom of Lake Swilly. There was an inquest where it was decided that the amount of lead in his backside acted essentially like an anchor, dragging him down to the bottom of the murky water and, therefore, the British government was responsible for his death. He was never seen again, much to Madge's relief.

Madge never took her eyes off people passing through the chapel gates. When everyone had passed by, she turned to Josie,

'Did you see who wasn't at mass?'

'Sure, if they weren't at mass, how could I see them not being there?'

Madge tutted,. 'Lila Hegarty! It's not like her to commit a mortal sin. Well, not one that people can see, anyway.'

Just then, Maura, a very attractive woman in her late fifties, came out of the chapel door arm in arm with her new husband. As they approached the gate, Maura saw Madge, who slows her pace and says lovingly to her husband,

'When we get home, darling, I'm going to make you your favourite bacon and eggs.' Ignoring Madge, she threw Josie a sweet smile. And sauntered past.

'Did you ever, in the whole of your life, see such a brazen hussy?' Madge was outraged.

'Imagine going into the house of God with her third husband and not one of the other two dead!'

'I know, Madge.' Josie shook her head. 'It's not fair. She got three husbands and you didn't even get one. But, don't you worry now, every day I say a prayer to Saint

Jude, he is the patron saint of impossible causes, that you'll get one before you die.'

Madge stormed off, leaving Josie, who was impervious to her gaff, to trot after her.

Chapter Three

Liam was checking out the Monday races. He wanted to do another accumulator on six races in the desperate hope of winning enough money to buy the pub. But he was constantly distracted by Soupy's loud, out-of-tune singing.

Liam looked up from the paper. 'Shut up, man!'

But Soupy was lost in the words of the song. He continued singing, 'I can fly higher than an eagle, for you are the… ' he raised one bum cheek from the stool and let out a loud, smelly fart, '… Wind beneath my feet.'

'You're drunk at eleven o'clock on a Monday morning! Do you never sober up?'

'I do not, Liam. Sobering up only gives you a hangover.'

Liam waved the newspaper in front of his nose in a vain attempt to get rid of the foul smell. 'Come on, Soupy, get your arse off that chair. I'll not tell you again!'

'That's five times you told me you wouldn't tell me again. Make your fecking mind up!'

Soupy broke into song again. Liam came out from behind the bar and grabbed him by the collar. 'Smart Alec, eh!'

'Would you hold your horses there and give a man the time to look his best?' He spits on his dirty hands and runs them through his matted hair. 'When you threw me out last night I had the good fortune to land on top of Biddley Boyle. She was inbetween clients so she didn't bother getting up. I'll tell you, sir, that woman's bosoms have more bounce than any trampoline.'

'You're a dirty wee bastard. You should be praying for a happy death!' Liam grabbed hold of Soupy's arm, but he broke free.

'I'll go under my own steam if you'll have the decency to point me in the right direction. For what better place could a man be resting than nestled between Biddley's Mountains.'

Liam turned Soupy and pointed him in the direction of the door. He staggered out past Bosco, who was on his way in.

'I'll have my usual.' Bosco sat on his stool looking flustered. 'And make it a double.' Liam poured a whiskey and watched Bosco gulp it down.

'Same again.'

'Two doubles?' Liam whistled under his breath. 'Either you won on the horses or someone has died.'

'You're right.' He swallowed the second whiskey. 'Give me another one.' His hand shook as he threw the whiskey down his throat.

'How much did you win?'

'Higs is dead!' Bosco put the empty glass down on the bar.

'Higs is dead?' Liam was both confused and stunned.

'As a doornail!' Bosco wiped his mouth.

'But… he was in the best of health when I left him home the other night.'

'Aye, well, there you are, you see,' Bosco sighed. 'Good health is no guarantee against dying. He was found at the bottom of the stairs.'

'God, the fall down the stairs killed him?'

'No!' He died at the top of the stairs from a hatchet blow to the back of the head. His wife is in custody. I hear she's claiming temporary insanity,' Bosco smirked. 'She'll never get off on that plea. Her and insanity have long been on intimate terms!'

'Jesus! That's horrific… We'll never see Higs again! Just shows you, we never know what's in front of us.'

'Or behind us!'

Liam poured himself a drink. 'I can't believe it.'

'Nor can I.' Bosco tried to squeeze out a tear. 'There will never be another one like him. I'll have another double in his memory.'

'I'll close the bar and we'll all attend the funeral.'

'Are you mad! Higs would be turning in his grave if he thought he was responsible for the bar being closed. No!' Bosco was adamant. 'I'll go as your emissary. I'll bring all the mourners back here and we'll have a bit of a "Do," as a mark of respect to our dear friend.'

'He asked if he could stay at mine the other night.' Liam swallowed a whiskey. 'If I'd let him stay, he'd still be alive.'

'Don't blame yourself, now. As my sainted mother used to say, if you're meant to be cleaved with a hatchet, you'll never be drowned in the bath. My mother had a wonderful way with words.'

'I heard Lila is a bit of a handlin. But to actually murder him!'

''tis hard to believe, all right.' Bosco reasoned, 'I mean, what harm did he do except go out for a drink on a Friday night, and a Saturday night and a Monday night, and a Tuesday and Wednesday night? Didn't he stay home every Thursday to keep her company and that's the thanks he got for it! Selfish bitch!'

Liam asked, 'What's wrong with people these days?'

'Aye, the world is up the left, all right. I remember the good ol' days when people were normal. We had rules you could depend on. We went to the pub on a Saturday night, got drunk, came home, ate Sunday dinner, wrecked the house and went to bed. That was before the Troubles. I blame them for the breakdown of family life. Before the Troubles, a man was master of his castle, ruler of his domestic domain. Then the fight for freedom started and everything went to hell. If you lifted your hand to the wife, she'd go to the Provos and they would come round and blow your balls off. Aye, women got ahead of themselves, and look where it ended.' Bosco banged his fist down hard on the bar. 'Men starting changing nappies and pushing prams! Now, they're wearing perfume and make-up.'

Liam looked at his watch. 'Oh shit! I have an appointment in Derry I can't miss. Can you hold the fort for me for an hour?'

'Aye, go ahead, but the Mrs will have the dinner ready at six and I daren't be late.'

Liam pulled on his jacket as he was leaving. He stopped at the door. 'By the way, I know how much whiskey is left in that bottle.'

Chapter Four

The noise from the industrial sewing machines was both deafening and neverending. Piles of high-visibility garments littered the long tables attached to each sewing machine. The women who worked in the factory were mostly married and middle-aged. Plus one lone male machine mechanic. Maureen's machine was situated opposite Shantel's. They had been friends since childhood. Now in their mid-twenties, they were both still single. The good friends had next to nothing in common. Shantel had bleached blond hair and a voluptuous figure. She was suntanned to within an inch of her life. Her personality matched her looks exactly. Maureen, on the other hand, was a tiny size six, with long hair as black as coal, and creamy skin that made her dark brown eyes look enormous.

Shantel was leaning over her machine all starry-eyed talking to Barry the mechanic. 'I didn't see you at the pub on Saturday night.' She leant a little more forward so that Barry had a good view of her cleavage.'

Barry's eyes fell to her breasts. He looked up, giving her a devastating smile. 'That's because I wasn't there.'

Curious to know where he'd been but not wanting to sound too interested, she tried to sound casual, 'So, where were you then?'

'I was on a date with a gorgeous Polish babe.'

Shantel moved away. 'And what would a gorgeous babe of any nationality be doing with the likes of you?'

Barry looked at her with a smirk on his face. 'You jealous?' He put his tools back into his belt and walked away.

Shantel called after him, 'In your dreams!' She swung around in a huff and bumped into Bridget, the supervisor, who had been there listening to the exchange.

'Maybe you could actually do some work now?' Bridget walked off. Shantel tried to bite her tongue.

'I'll... ef... ef... '

'Don't say it!'

'Bitch! Someday I'm going to punch her lights out!' She sat down at her machine and started to sew a garment.

'There's Karaoke in Murphy's Pub tonight,' Maureen said casually. 'What about calling in for an hour? You never know who you might there... '

'In Murphy's Pub!' Shantel pretends to throw up. 'That's the last stop before oblivion. After the last time we were there I told you I wouldn't be caught dead in it again!'

Maureen pretended to be absorbed in the garment she was sewing. 'I heard Barry telling Bridget he is going to be singing there. You know how he likes to show off.'

'You're only saying that so I'll go with you.'

'Oh, shut up! Are you going or not?'

Shantel heaved a sigh of resignation. Maureen had been trying to get Liam to notice her for ages and Shantel was dragged along almost every week to sit in that dump with the golden oldies.

'All right, then. But if Barry's not there, I'm leaving!'

Liam had been waiting outside the bank manager's office for almost an hour and he was getting impatient. Finally, the office door opened and a very attractive woman came out, smiling at him,

'Mr Doherty? The manager will see you now. Just follow me, please.'

Liam followed her into a very upscale office. The bank manager was sitting at an enormous desk reading something on one of the two computers in front of him. For the first few minutes, he totally ignored Liam's presence. Finally, after what seemed like forever, he looked at Liam over the rim of his glasses.

'So, Mr Doherty,' hed looks back at the computer, obviously reading Liam's application form, 'I see you're asking the bank for a loan of fifty thousand pounds? That's quite a considerable chunk of money. How would you pay it back?'

'With money, just like anyone else.'

'I see. So, you are in a position to repay the bank? And how would you do that?' He looked through the form. 'You don't seem to have collateral of any kind?'

Liam shifted uncomfortably in his seat. 'Well, not at the moment.'

'Perhaps you're expecting someone to die and leave you an inheritance?' The manager stared at Liam, one eyebrow raised.

'I'm a bar manager, have been for more than ten years. The bar manages a decent gross yearly income. I don't see a problem repaying the loan.'

'Mr Doherty, you have no assets to speak of. Therefore, you cannot offer any guarantee that the bank would get its money back. You don't even have a savings account with us either…'

Liam lost his cool. 'So, you're telling me that the only way you'll give me a loan is if I can prove to you that I don't fucking need it!'

Liam was escorted out of the bank wedged between two burly security guards. He pulled his arms away from their grasp. 'Take your hands off me!'

One of the security guards poked his finger hard against Liam's ribs. 'Don't come back here again unless you want to be wearing your arse at the front!'

Liam walked away totally dejected, muttering to himself, 'Well, that's that then. Bastard!'

Madge and Josie came into the pub. Liam put down the glasses he was drying.

'Good day, ladies.'

'I'll have my usual,' Madge snaps.

'A vodka and milk it is…'

'I don't drink vodka and milk, I drink milk and vodka. Pour the milk first and then the vodka.' She stared at Josie. 'Well, get your money out.'

'Seeing as how I'm paying, I'll have a sherry.'

'Give her half a sherry, I'm not going to be left with a legless drunk tonight again!' Madge took her drink to her usual chair in the corner and sat down. Josie turned to Liam.

'Stick a wee extra drop in my glass. Do you know Higs is dead? Madge has been in great form since she heard the news.'

They both look across at Madge who was humming into her glass.

Bosco's wife, Margie, was talking to neighbours over her garden fence. The subject of conversation was, of course, Higs's demise.

'He got what was coming to him, it's just a pity he de didn't get it years ago!' Margie crossed her arms. 'That man was nothing but a lay-a-bout. I'll tell you something for nothing, it'll give the men in this village something to think about. Including that bastard I married!'

'The undertaker told our Jean that the body was in a terrible state.' Cassie lowered her voice. 'Apparently, she sliced his head right down the middle of his face with a hatchet!'

'Well, that one long eyebrow of his will be finally separated for the funeral,' Margie replied with some satisfaction.

'I heard that Lila Hegarty's solicitor is trying to get her out on bail so she can sleep in her own bed until the trial.' Annie added. 'But the judge said no chance. Poor Lila is staying locked up. And, another thing, who's going to wake him? Sure, he hasn't a relative left above the ground.'

Margie said, 'They can take him from the morgue to the cemetery; it's no more than what he deserves.'

'You are dead right, Margie,' Cassie responded. 'I think we should hold a protest outside the police station to demand Lila's release.'

Maureen came around the corner and shouted at her mother, 'Is my lunch ready? I have to be back at work in half an hour.'

'It's on the kitchen table.' Margie turned to go inside but turned back to Cassie.

'I think you might be right about that march, Cassie. It's time the men in this town were taught a lesson.'

Chapter Five

A very old hearse chugged up the steep hill that leads to Saint Joseph's Catholic Church. When it reached the top, it turned slowly through the heavy wrought-iron gates and came to a stop at a side door just out of view of the street. Ninety- three-year-old Egbert McClafferty and his seventy- three-year-old son, Egbert Junior, struggled to get out of the ancient car. Junior went to the back of the hearse and opened the double doors. Father Divine had been waiting anxiously for their arrival. He hurried out of the parochial house.

'You are running somewhat late. Mass will be starting in forty minutes. I trust you will not linger long in the chapel?'

'Good day to you, Father Devine.' Egbert senior shook the Priest's hand. 'Don't worry now, we'll be gone before you know it. Okay, son, get the trolley.'

'Trolley?' Father Divine was confused.

Egbert Senior explained, 'It's just a wee thing I threw together to lend us a hand. Junior isn't getting any younger, you know.' Junior pulled what looked like a four-wheeled, plywood stretcher with springs, out from beside the coffin. He set it on the ground, then slowly raised it to the level of the hearse floor. Standing at each side of the coffin, the two Egberts began, very slowly, to pull the coffin out. All went well until they got it on the trolley. Suddenly, there was a loud snap and one of the wheels came off and rolled past the Priest's feet.

'I think you might need to make a new trolley, Daddy.'

The coffin tilted to one side and began to slide off. Father and son made a lunge for it to catch it. Father Divine didn't move. He stood watching them with his arms folded.

'How do you feel about giving us a hand, Father?' There was a hint of sarcasm in Egbert Senior's voice.

'Right.' Father Divine was not impressed but had no choice but to help them.

'Don't you worry now, Father, we'll have him inside in no time.'

Between the three of them, they managed to get Higs inside the chapel. All they needed to do now was lift the coffin onto the stand in front of the small altar.

'Right,' Egbert Senior said. 'On the count of three, we'll raise the coffin up level with the stand and then slide it on. Okay?'

'Will you hurry up?' Father Divine was breathless. 'I think I'm going to faint!'

'One...' They start to lift the coffin higher. 'Two...' It was almost level with the stand. 'Three!'

They slid it along from the back end of the stand towards the front, but they misjudged the distance and the coffin fell over the other end, landing on the floor on its head.

'Oh, dear!' Egbert Senior assessed the damage. 'It's all right now, he didn't escape. But I'm thinking he'll not know which end of him is up.'

'No change there then,' Junior remarked. 'When he was living he could never figure out if it was a shite or a haircut he needed.'

'May I remind you that you are in the house of God!'

'Very sorry now, Father.' Junior looked remorseful. 'I'll say three Hail Marys at bedtime.'

'See that you do.' Father Divine looked at his watch. 'The mass will be starting in twenty-five minutes. I trust you will have things sorted and be out of the chapel by then.'

'We'll do our best to make him presentable. But, after his encounter with that hatchet, we might need you to pray for a miracle.'

Junior unscrewed the coffin lid and looked in at Higs. 'Even a miracle wouldn't help him, Daddy. He was born an ugly bastard and he died an ugly bastard.'

'Forget about the three Hail Marys. Say fifteen decades of the Rosary.' Father Divine turned on his heel and left the chapel.

Chapter Six

Liam had the newspaper spread out on the top of the bar checking the runners in the afternoon races. Soupy was sitting at the bar, twiddling his dirty thumbs and humming under his breath. The only other two customers who were in the pub were Corky Gillespie and his wheelchair, with his pal, Blinkers Bradley, who was totally blind. Bosco hurried in and gave a nod to them. He ordered a drink.

'You look a bit through, yourself.' Liam poured him a drink. 'Has someone else died?'

'The women are organising a protest march to the police station to try and get that woman out of jail! Can you believe it?'

'You better believe it!' Corky shouted. 'The march doesn't start till five o'clock and our John's Mrs left hours ago so she would be in the front row. And she made no dinner for him! Nor me!' Bosco swallowed the second drink and slid the empty glass along the bar to Liam.

'Imagine. The cheek of them women trying to get a murderer out of jail! It's a sad state of affairs when a man gets murdered by his wife in his own home and she's considered the martyr. I think we should have a counter march to get Higs out of the chapel and give him a decent Irish wake!'

'And where is he going to be waked?' Liam asked. 'There's not a woman in this town who'll let Higs over her doorstep.'

'It's not good enough, I tell you. Not good enough!' Bosco wiped some sweat from his temple with the cuff of his jacket.

'Aye, it's very sad,' Soupy piped up. 'He must be lonely laying up in that empty chapel with not a living soul to keep him company on his last day on earth. Right, I'll see you later. Luck now.' He stepped out of the pub and bumped into Biddley. 'Biddley, you're looking well, as usual.' Biddley had holes in her tights, lipstick on her nose and what looked like the branch of a tree stuck in her hair.

'Soupy, pet, I was just looking for you. I'm a bit hungry. How about if you buy me a big greasy bag of chips?'

'Sure, wouldn't I do anything for you, Biddley?'

Ten minutes later, they were sitting on the footpath eating the chips. Soupy reached into his pocket, pulled out a hat and slapped it on his head.

'Do you like it?' He adjusted the hat and smiled at her. 'It was Higs's. I found it lying outside his house. I put it on my head to keep it warm for him.'

'Where he's going he won't need any help keeping warm.'

'Come on, wee girl, we'll give him back his hat now.'

Biddley and Soupy were hiding behind a bush, in the grounds of the chapel. Soupy's head popped up amongst the leaves as he checked for passers-by. '

It's okay, the coast is clear.'

Biddley's head popped up beside his. She was holding a small pair of binoculars to her eyes.

'Where did you get them things?'

'Last night, I got a new client. He did the deed and then refused to pay me so I wrestled these binoculars from around his neck. He was devastated. He's a peeping Tom, you see.' She raised them to her eyes again and scanned the area.

'C'mon now, before somebody comes.' Soupy emerged cautiously from behind the bush.

'Look, Soupy, I think I'll wait out here. If the Blessed Virgin saw me in there, she'd faint.'

'Right. I'll not be long.' He ran from behind the bush and disappeared inside the chapel. The chapel was deserted and deathly quiet, with only the occasional sound of a passing car. Soupy walked up the long centre aisle on his tiptoes to where the open coffin sat. He stood looking down at Higs. A single teardrop escaped and rolled down his cheek.

'I've come to give you back your cap.' He took the cap from his head and put it gently on Higs's deformed skull. 'There, now, you look like the Higs we all know and love.' A tray of candles flickered softly on the altar. Soupy reached into his pockets searching for a coin but they were empty. He did a quick scan of the chapel to check that he was alone before reaching into the candle box and stealing one. He lit it from one of the lighted candles and bows his head in prayer.

'Lord, take Higs into Heaven. I know he was a bit of a chancer but, you see, Lord, the temptation of the drink was too much for him. He was a weak man. A bit like myself, God help me. Oh, aye, and you know he had an eye for the ladies. But, sure, it was only a bit of craic.' Lost in prayer, he didn't realise the candle had set his hair alight. At that exact moment, Father Divine walked out onto the altar.

'I hope you paid for that candle!'

Soupy felt the heat and realised his hair was on fire. 'Oh, shit!' He rushed to the baptismal font and dunked his head in the holy water. When he was sure the fire was out, he lifted his head back up and looked at Father Divine, who was horrified at the sight of holy water dripping over Soupy's dirty jacket.

'Sorry, now, Father, that just slipped out. Isn't the Devil just everywhere!'

'That's two mortal sins you've committed. Stealing and blaspheming in the house of God! I shall expect to see you at confession on Saturday night.'

'I'll be there, Father.' He genuflected respectfully to the priest. 'Um, what time is confession at?'

'Seven o'clock. The same as it's been for the past seventy years. If you weren't a heathen, you'd know that.' Father Divine stormed from the altar. Soupy waited for a few seconds to be sure the priest was gone. And when he was sure he was alone again, he rushed over and dunked his head back in the holy water.

Madge and Josie got on the bus. They took their seats beside Linda and her sister, Debra. 'Did you hear about Higs… '

Madge butted in, 'I've heard about nothing else. The way people are carrying on you'd think it was the Pope who died!' She turned to Josie. 'Have you got your post office card with you?'

'I have, Madge. I put it inside my knickers so I wouldn't forget it.'

Debra spoke up, 'Did you hear Lila took an electric drill and halted his body down the middle? By all accounts, he fell in two different directions.'

Madge smirked. 'Good enough for the bastard, that's what I say!' Josie started to fidget around in the seat.

'Oh, dear!'

'What is it now?' Madge snapped.

'I think I have to pee.'

Madge stood up and pulled Josie up by the arm. 'C'mon, before there's a flash flood in here.' They arrived at the post office to find the closed sign on the door. Madge looked at her watch.

'It's only half-four. She can't close at this time!' Madge knocked with some force on the door a number of times. Eventually, it was opened by Nora, the post mistress. Madge didn't give her a chance to speak. 'What's the meaning of the post office being closed at half-four? Some of us need our pension money.'

Josie was jumping up and down now. 'Can I use your toilet, quick?'

'Not a bother, Josie, c'mon with me.' Nora opened a side door and showed Josie through to the ladies room. She returned almost immediately. 'Well, Madge, what can I do for you?'

'Just give me twenty pounds. I need to buy spuds and bread and I want ten pounds worth of electricity. Isn't the price of electricity shocking? All my mother had to light the house was a couple of oil lamps. And weren't we just as well off.'

Josie returned from the toilet looking relieved. She smiled warmly at Nora. 'That was grand. I feel better now.'

'I hope you squeezed it all out!' Madge wagged her finger at Josie. 'Because I'm not stopping at every toilet between here and home.'

Josie reached into her bag and took out her card. She gave it to Nora. 'Forty pounds, please… '

'What! What do you want forty pounds for?' She turns to Nora. 'Give her ten.'

Nora looks at Josie. 'Okay, Josie?'

'Aye, sure, that's grand.'

Nora handed the money to Josie with her card. 'Well, if there's nothing else, I'll just lock the door behind you. The march will be starting soon and I don't want to miss it.'

'Can I go with you?' Josie asked. 'It's a long time since I was on a good march. What are we marching for?'

'It's the "Free The Tullaghmoragh One" march. We're demanding that they let Lila Hegarty out of jail on bail so she can sleep in her own bed.'

'We're going to no march! This is Bingo night. As far as I'm concerned Lila Hegarty can stay where she is.' Madge elbowed Josie. 'Go on, move.'

'I'll see you later, Nora. I might be at the march. There could be a bomb scare at the Bingo hall. You never know.'

"You're thirty years behind the times, Josie! The British surrendered thirty years ago.' Nora followed them to the door and locked it behind them.

'Right. I'm out of here.' Shantel threw the garment she was sewing to one side. Maureen looked at her watch.

'But, it's only quarter-to-five.'

'I just saw Bridget the bitch leave so we're in the clear. C'mon, I'll have plenty of time to do your makeup.

Maureen grabbed her coat and bag and they walked quickly to the back door. 'What are you wearing tonight?'

'I was thinking my red miniskirt,' Shantel replied. 'What are you wearing?' They disappeared through the door.

Maude was with her husband sitting on a bench in their front garden enjoying a pleasant autumn day. Madge and Josie walked towards them. Madge saw them first, her back stiffened. She took hold of Josie's arm in an attempt to pull her across to the other side of the street before Josie sees them. But it was too late.

'Oh, look, Madge, it's Maude and her new husband.'

Madge tried to push Josie away but she had a firm hold on Maude's garden fence. 'Let go of that fence this minute!'

Josie ignored Madge and shouted a greeting to Maude, 'How're you, Maude?'

'I'm very well, Josie.'

'Sure, that's grand, what is your latest husband's name?'

Maude hooked her arm through her husband's and kissed him affectionally on the cheek. 'This is Peter. Peter, meet Josie and Madge.' She gave her husband a knowing glance. 'Remember I told you about her?'

'Ah, yes, hello, ladies.' Peter had a distinctive English accent.

Josie asks, 'Are you a foreigner?'

'Of course, he's a foreigner,' Madge retorted. 'There's not an Irish man left she hasn't married.' Maude smiled sweetly at Madge.

'Peter might have a rusty cousin laying around somewhere that no one is using. Play your cards right, Madge, and I'll get you fixed up with him.'

Madge's face turned purple with rage. She pried Josie's hand off the fence. 'C'mon you!'

She hurried down the street with Josie lagging behind. Maude's laughter echoed down the street after them.

Chapter Seven

Soupy and Bosco sat quietly at the bar. The television was on but the volume was muted. Corky and his drinking buddy, Ding, sat in the corner having a noisy discussion about football.

'Hey, Liam,' Corky calls. 'Who won the nineteen-forty-six world cup?'

'There was no world cup that year. It didn't start again until nineteen-fifty.'

'Told you.' Corky slapped Ding's back. 'I'll have a pint, Liam, and it's on him.'

Liam took two pints to the table and took the money from a reluctant Ding.

The faint sound of cheers filtered into the pub, followed by spontaneous clapping and singing.

Bosco asked, 'What's that?' He went outside to investigate and, a few seconds, he shouted for Liam to come outside. Liam walked leisurely out of the pub to the street.

'Look at that!' Bosco pointed to the marchers. 'I can't believe my eyes!'

A few hundred women were marching along the street towards the village square. Some of them were carrying homemade placards with various derogatory comments about Higs. A huge banner led the march carried by a woman on each side.

'The wives have had enough. It's about time we got tough!' Another woman was carrying a banner with a painting of a hatchet with blood dripping from it. When the march reached the pub it came to a sudden halt. One of the marchers shouted at the top of her voice,

'Liberty for Lila! Free the Tullamoragh One!' The women shouted in unison, 'Free Lila now!' Annie stepped forward and pointed to Murphy's Pub.

'That's the den of iniquity where Higs spent all his time and money!'

'I'ts where that man I'm married to spends all his money too!' Cassie shouted. 'There's not a penny left for me to play bingo.'

'There'll be no sex tonight!' the woman cheered loudly.

'Thank God for small mercies.' Bosco didn't notice his wife, Margie, until she stepped out from the crowd. 'Margie, dear,' he stammered. 'I didn't know you were marching.'

Margie raised her homemade placard high above her head and slapped it down hard on Bosco's skull. He fell to the ground and a cheer went up from the marchers.

Margie looked down at her husband. 'Well, you know now, don't you?'

A random voice rang out from the crowd, 'Lila Hegarty shouldn't be in jail. She should be canonised!'

'That's right,' someone else shouted. 'Only a saint could put up with that man she married. He was nothing but a drunken bastard. She should have killed him years ago!'

Liam helped Bosco to his feet amid roars of laughter from the women. The march took off again along the street nearly causing a serious accident when two bicycles going in opposite directions crashed head-on.

Liam helped Bosco back up to his feet. 'Jesus, Bosco! You better watch your back. You could be next! Come on in, have a drink on me.'

'Aye, thanks, Liam.' Bosco straightened his coat. 'Make it a double.'

The march made its way onto O'Connell Street, where the police station was located.

Police patrol partners, Michael and Maurice, were on foot patrol in a side street. They stopped at the fish and chip shop for their favourite meal; a battered sausage supper. Michael was happily single with no intention of changing his status anytime soon. After all, why should he? He had a number of women on the go.

Maurice, on the other hand, had been married to Prindy for eight years. He told everyone what a great wife she was and how he never goes out socially without her because he doesn't want her to feel lonely. The truth was she didn't allow him to go out unless she was with him.

Maurice shoved a whole sausage into his mouth. 'There's nothing like a battered sausage to keep the hunger pains at bay.'

'Will it not spoil Prindy's dinner?' Michael shoved a few chips in his mouth. 'You could get in trouble.'

'Oh, God, Duffy, hold your tongue. I would be in big trouble if she knew what I ate when I'm working. She is on a gluten-free, vegetarian, no carbs diet, so she said I'm on it too. I'm that hungry I could eat the legs of the table.' He hungrily ate the other sausage.

'Another good reason for me to stay single! I can eat what I like, drink when I like, and… well, you know, do the other thing that I like.'

The sound of loud voices in the distance reached them.

'Sounds like a disturbance to me.' Maurice threw his empty sausage container in a bin. Duffy threw his on the ground. They hurried in the direction of the voices. And, turning a corner onto O'Connell Street, they met the marchers head-on. When the women saw the two policemen, they became restless. Duffy's eyes quickly scanned the banner. When he saw a placard with Lila Hegarty's name on it, he froze.

'Oh, dear.'

Lecky said, I don't like the looks of this. They look annoyed.' Lecky stepped behind Duffy. 'What are you going to do?'

A woman at the front of the march overheard him. She rollsed up her sleeves and squared up to Duffy.

'Aye, what are you going to do about it?'

Duffy sized up the situation and made a life-saving decision. 'Not a thing.' He gave a nervous cough. 'Right.

Lecky, we need to get back to work.' Duffy swung around on his heel and walked away. Lecky hesitated.

The woman stared at Lecky. 'Maybe you want to do something about it?'

Lecky said, 'Oh, no, definitely not!' He backed away and hurried after Duffy.

Duffy and Lecky headed in the same direction as they came. They took a shortcut back to the police station. 'Don't tell anyone in the station that we ran into those marchers.' Duffy looked behind him nervously. 'I don't want them to know that we were scared off by a bunch of women!'

Sergeant O'Doherty was at work at the front desk of the police station, blissfully unaware of the chaos that was about to descend on the street outside. Sergeant O'Doherty was a man of a thin build, with thinning grey hair and a face that is, well, lived in. He was known amongst his fellow police colleagues as a man who avoided conflict at any cost. Hence his nickname, Butter Balls. Duffy and Lecky arrived at the station both looking flustered.

Sergeant O'Doherty looked up from the computer. "So, you're back? Any incidents? Anything to report? You look like you've been running?"

'Running? No!' Duffy took his hat off. 'It's just a bit hot out there. Isn't that right, Lecky?'

'That's right, Sarg.' Lecky took a hankie from his pocket and fanned himself in an exaggerated way. 'It's very hot outside, so it is.'

'Right, well, get your paperwork done. I've a few things I need you to do before you go off-duty and take my wife to lunch.'

Just then, the heavy front door flew open and Sergeant O'Doherty's wife rushed into the station. She shouted at her husband, 'Paddy! There's a march coming down the road, hundreds of women. And they look angry!'

'What? What are you talking about!' The Sergeant thumbed through the daily records. 'There's no record here of anyone applying for a permit to march.'

'They look like they don't give a fu… damn about any marching permit.' She looked out of the window. 'It's something to do with Lila Hegarty!'

'That bloody woman has caused nothing but bother.' The Sergeant sat down. 'Forty years she's been married to him and now she decides to murder him. Why the hell couldn't she have waited two more years and I'd be retired!'

Duffy and Lecky tried to get out unnoticed.

'And where do you think you two are going?'

'We were just going to have a wee cuppa. It's been a long day, Sarg.' Duffy looked tense.

'You two stay where you are.' He tried not to sound nervous. 'We need all hands on deck.' The sound of chanting and singing mixed with cheers could be heard in the distance.

'Lecky, get out there and see how far away they are.' The Sergeant wiped his brow with a nervous hand.

'Right, Sarg.' Lecky went outside and immediately ran back in. 'They're not twenty yards away! The television cameras are following them. I think there could be a riot!'

'There'll be no riot here. Not on my watch! They need to be put straight about the law.' The Sergeant sat down again. 'Lecky, go out there and explain the law to them.'

Lecky protested, 'But, Sarg. They're not going to listen to me.'

'That's a direct order!'

'Right, Sarg.' Lecky took a few steps towards the door. 'How about if I tell them to come back tomorrow and we can all call in sick?'

Duffy peeked out of the window. 'Oh, somehow I don't think they're going to agree to that.' Lecky stepped out of the station and was met with a chorus of jeers.

The sound of "Free The Tullaghmore One!" was deafening.

Someone shouted, 'Lila Hegarty shouldn't be in jail for killing that bastard. She should be canonised for putting up with him for all them years!'

Secure in the knowledge that the gate to the station was locked, Lecky stepped forward. 'Um… Ladies! Ladies, please. You need to go home and let us do our jobs. The law clearly states that anyone involved in an illegal march will be prosecuted to the fullest extent of the law.'

A balloon filled with water smashed into his face, soaking his hair and the front of his uniform. The women gave a hearty cheer. Egged on by some women at the back of the march, the women on the front line grabbed the gate and tried to force it open.

Clearly spooked, Lecky slowly backed away from the crowd and hurried into the police station. 'I told you they wouldn't listen to me, Sergeant. They're out for blood.'

Duffy looked over his shoulder. 'Aye, ours!'

The Sergeant realised he was backed into a corner. 'Okay. Duffy, Lecky, come out with me. I'll talk to them. Duffy, give me the megaphone.'

Duffy asked, 'What are you going to say to them?'

'Fucked, if I know!' The Sergeant threw his shoulders back. He turned to his wife. 'Betty, do not come outside no matter what happens.' He went outside, followed very reluctantly by Duffy and Lecky. When they saw Sergeant O'Doherty, the women became more agitated and began to chant,

'Free the Tullaghmore one! Justice for Lila Hegarty!'

'Ladies, please. Can we be quiet so I can speak?'

"Quiet down, everyone," Margie told the crowd. 'Let's hear what he has to say.'

A lull came over the marchers as they waited to hear what the Sergeant had to say. He took a deep breath and did his best to speak with some authority.

'I understand your loyalty to your friend, it's very noble of all of you. But Mrs Hegarty murdered her husband for no apparent reason, and without provocation.'

'Aye, up yours!' Cassie called. 'How would you know that? You're sticking up for him because he's a man. If he had murdered Lila, you would let him out on bail, you skinny-looking bastard!'

'I don't think they're going to listen to you.' Duffy took a big step away from the Sergeant. With the megaphone to his mouth, he uttered the fatal words, 'I'm going to ask you all to leave. This is an illegal march. You are blocking traffic and behaving in a threatening manner!'

His attempts to continue talking were drowned out by the volume of boos coming from the marchers.

Duffy stated, "It's not looking good, Sarg.'

'Oh, you think! Get inside and call for reinforcements! Now!'

Chapter Eight

Back in Murphy's Pub, Bosco sat at the bar nursing the beginning of a black eye.

Liam poured a whiskey. 'It's on the house.' He set it in front of Bosco. 'I didn't know you were a battered husband.'

Bosco threw the whiskey back and slammed the empty glass on the bar. 'That's the first time the wife has lifted her hand to me. Higs's wife didn't just murder him, she put the rest of us in mortal danger!'

'You could always get a divorce.'

'I would except I forgot to get her to sign a prenup. There's no way she's getting her greedy hands on my football cards. I've been collecting them since the sixties. They're worth a few bob.' Bosco sighed deeply. 'I don't know where it's all going to end.'

'On television!'

'What?'

Liam turned the volume up. The march had turned into a riot and was being broadcast live. The camera scanned the crowd as a reporter's voice-over could be heard detailing what was happening,

'The peaceful march turned into a riot when the marchers were told that Lila Hegarty, was the number one suspect in the murder of her husband, one Kevin Barry Hegarty.' As the camera continued to pan the crowd, Margie suddenly came into view. The camera stayed with her as she took a tomato from her bag and threw it with some force at the Sergeant's face. It was a bull's eye, smashing into his nose and dripping down over his mouth and onto his pristine white shirt.

'Oh, my God!' Bosco was horrified. 'Did you see that?'

'The whole of Ireland just saw that.' Liam poured another whiskey for Bosco. 'Looks like you and your Mrs could be keeping Lila company in her cell.'

'How could she be so bloody stupid! She knows the police have been looking for me for outstanding fines. They think I live in Derry. Now I'm not going to be able to stay in my own house. The place with be crawling with cops. I need somewhere to hide.'

The camera was now focused on the reporter, but in the background the police could be seen taking a handful of women into custody.

'Would you put me up?' he pleaded. 'Just for one night, please, Liam? You could be saving my life!'

Liam turned the television off. 'Right, you can stay for one night only.'

'Good man, yourself.' Bosco got down from his stool. 'I'll run home now and get a change of clothes. Hopefully, before the police get there. If I don't come back, get me a solicitor.' Bosco rushed out of the pub, almost bumping into Madge and Josie. He turned quickly in the opposite direction.

'You better watch yourself, Bosco Brown,' Madge called after him. 'Your wife was seen in B&Q looking at hatchets.'

Bosco hurried to the nearest taxi stand and jumped into one that was about to pull away. 'Thirty-five Racecourse Road, as quick as you can.'

The taxi driver turned around to look at Bosco. 'I'm on my way to pick up a fare. Get out!'

'Look, I'll give you a fiver extra.' Bosco pulled the money out of his pocket and threw it at the driver. 'Okay?'

'Okay, but this is against my moral principles.' The driver tucked the fiver in his pocket and drove off. Three minutes later, they arrive at Bosco's house. 'That'll be eight--ifty.'

'Eight fifty! That means I paid you thirteen-fifty for one mile. I just want you to know something. Dick Turpin had the decency to wear a mask!' Bosco looked out of the taxi window. There was no sign of Margie or the police. He jumped out of the taxi and hurried into the house. Fifty seconds later, he was on his way back out. He reached for the door handle when it was flung open and hit him in the face.

Margie asked, 'Where do you think you're going with them clothes?'

"Jesus! You broke my nose!' Blood poured down his nostrils. He went to the kitchen to get a tissue to stop the blood. When he was there, he grabbed a Tesco bag and shoved his clothes in it.

'Did you hear what I said? Where are you going?'

Bosco replied, 'I'm going on the run. I can't believe you threw a tomato at a police sergeant!'

'Get your facts right. It was a rotten tomato!'

'They'll be here in a minute to arrest you. And I'm not sticking around to get arrested for fines I have no bloody money to pay.' Bosco opened the door and rushed out.

Margie followed him outside and shouts after him, 'And don't come back!' She turned to go back into the house, when she saw the neighbourhood gossip peering through her window. 'What are you looking at!' The curtains pulled closed quickly. Annie came out from next door to see what all the shouting was about.

Annie said, 'I thought that was your voice I heard. What's wrong?' Margie called one final insult after Bosco's retreating frame,

'Bastard!'

'Right.' Annie put her arm around Margie. 'What about a cup of tea? C'mon.'

'Okay, but I'll need a drop of whiskey to bring me around.'

Annie replied, 'I put a wee drop for just such an occasion.' They went into Annie's house.

Bosco hurried along trying to look inconspicuous. Some men were across the street talking. One of them shouted across at him,

'Hey, Bosco, we saw your wife on the news. With an aim like that she should be playing for Celtic!' There was a big cheer from the other men.

Bosco gave them a half-hearted wave. He turned a corner, right into the path of Duffy and Lecky. Shaken, he hesitated for a few seconds before deciding to brazen it out. He began to whistle as he nonchalantly walked passed the policemen. He got about ten feet.

'Hold it! Where do you think you're going? Put your hands behind your back and don't move.' Duffy meant business. Bosco put his hands behind his back, closed his eyes and waited for the dreaded hand on the shoulder.

'We finally caught you after all these months!'

Resigned to his fate, Bosco turned around slowly to face the police, just in time to see them shove a scruffy-looking man into the patrol car. Bosco stood dazed, looking as the police car drove past him at speed. Adrenalin deserted him and he leant heavily against the wall for support.

Quietly, under his breath, he sayid, 'Thank you, Jesus.'

Bosco was back in the bar in his usual seat, on full alert should the police come in looking for him. Liam was behind the bar eating a takeaway. He took a mouthful and immediately spat it back into the container.

'My dog gets better food than this shite!' He binned the uneaten food.

Bosco said, 'What you need is a good woman who'll keep you well-fed.'

'My mother was a good woman and she couldn't cook to save her life. My father died from malnutrition.' Liam breathed a deep sigh. 'I have to give up the pub.'

'Give up the pub! Why would you give up the pub?'

'It's being sold. Apparently, O'Malley got an offer he can't refuse. So, that's it, I'm out of a job.' Liam poured himself a drink.

'Surely not. I mean, whoever buys it will need a good manager like you. They're bound to keep you on. Do you know who's buying it?'

'Some conglomerate from Belfast.'

Bosco is outraged. 'Oh, great! Some wanker from Belfast is going to take over our local and turn it into another trendy wine bar for teenage half-wits. Is there nothing you can do?'

'He's asking fifty thousand pounds. It's all I can do to pay the monthly bills... No, there's not a thing I can do about it.'

'What about a loan from the bank? You could ask them. Think about it. What are we all going to do if the pub goes? God, it doesn't bear thinking about. What a day this is turning out to be.'

'I already asked the bank and they turned me down flat.'

'Give me a double.' Bosco threw some change on the bar.

The door burst open and Soupy staggered in and threw his singed head on the bar top.

What happened to you?'

'It was divine intervention,' Soupy moaned. 'How does it look?'

Bosco replies, 'It looks painful.'

'My scalp feels like it's still on fire. I think I've lost ten layers of skin!' Liam poured a whiskey for Soupy.

'It's on the house.'

Soupy grabbed the glass and, with shaking hands, swallowed the contents. 'God bless you, Liam! I needed that. Oh, that's better, I can feel my hair growing back already. That's the first time I've been inside a chapel in thirty years. And it'll be another thirty before I set foot inside another one. Father Divine can kiss my arse!'

Chapter Nine

The Sergeant was booking in the criminal Duffy and Lecky arrested. Plus a very drunk Biddley who was standing in front of him swaying in a circular motion. Duffy, the arresting officer, was standing beside her, notebook at the ready.

The Sergeant looked at Duffy. 'What was it this time?'

'Shoplifting in the pound shop. She was caught outside the shop with the item in question. The manager doesn't want to press charges. He said it's not worth the bother.'

'He doesn't want to press charges because I might have a wee story to tell his wife.' Biddley gave the Sergeant an exaggerated wink.

'Do you not think you're getting a bit old for this game?'

'Aye, right enough, Sergeant O'Doherty. I can't run as fast as I used to.' Biddley was cautioned for the hundredth warning.

Shantel was finishing getting ready for a night in Murphy's Pub. She checked herself out in the mirror. Her black lace blouse was completely see-through revealing a lipstick-red bra underneath. It was a good match for the red, imitation leather miniskirt, which just about covered her backside. Satisfied with her appearance, she left the house. When she closed the door behind her, she suddenly hoped wearing five-inch heels wasn't a mistake. Cautiously, she tried to manoeuvre her way along the cracked pavement. She almost made it to the end of the street, when it happened. One of her heels sank down into a crack. It stuck, which caused her to fall forward on her hands and knees. Just then, a car came along and pulled up beside her. She looked up into the driver's face and was mortified to sees Barry smiling down at her.

'Your skirt is so short I can almost see what you had for dinner.'

Shantel struggled to get to her feet but her shoe stayed firmly stuck in the crack. She bent down to retrieve it. She vigorously pulled at the shoe, but it came away leaving the heel stuck in the mud.

'Shit!' Shantel bites her lip.

'Oh, dear.' Barry frowns. 'I would give you a lift but I've got a hot date with my gorgeous Polish babe. And she doesn't like to be kept waiting.' He gave her a knowing wink. 'Be careful you don't step on glass.' He drove off laughing. Shantel threw the broken shoe after the car and hobbled down the street.

Maureen was in her bedroom waiting impatiently. She looked at her watch and wondered if Shantel had changed her mind about going out, when she heard footsteps on the stairs. The door was suddenly flung open. Shantel hobbled in wearing her one good shoe.

'I only came to tell you that I'm not going out. Look at the state of me!' Maureen tried not to smile at the sight of her.

'What happened to you?'

'Look at me. I spent an hour putting fake tan on my legs. Now I look like I've been knee-capped.' Shantel flopped down on Maureen's bed.

Margie came into the bedroom. 'Did you skin your knees running after Barry? What time are you two going out? I want to say my Rosary.'

'We'll be out of here in a few minutes, Ma.'

Margie left the room and Shantel turned accusingly to Maureen. 'How does she know I fancy Barry!'

Maureen rolled her eyes. 'The whole town knows you fancy Barry.'

'I'm going home.' Shantel looked at her reflection in the mirror. 'God!'

'C'mon, I'll find you something to wear.' Maureen opened the wardrobe door and pulled out a pair of jeans. 'C'mon, you know you want to go.'

Margie sat in her favourite armchair patiently waiting for Maureen and Shantel to leave the house. She had her Rosary beads strategically placed on the arm of her chair. The living room door openede and Maureen peeked her head in.

'We're going now, Ma. I have my front door key.'

'Okay, enjoy yourselves, and don't get drunk.'

The front door closed behind them. Margie went to the window and watched as they walked down the street. When she was sure they'd gone, she made herself comfortable and searched through Netflix until she found the right film. Before she pressed play, she picked up her Rosary beads, blessed herself and, head bowed, prayed,

'God, please forgive me!' She relaxed back into her chair as the opening credits of Fifty Shades Of Grey began.

'Hello, Margie!' Annie shouted from the hallway. 'Are you there?'

In her panic to turn the television off, she dropped the remote control and it slid under the chair. She got down on the floor, her fingers fumbled around in a wasted attempt to retrieve the control. Annie came in and saw Margie stretched on the carpet.

'Margie! Are you all right?'

Margie seized the opportunity to get Annie out of the room. 'Oh, Annie, could you get me a drink of water, please?'

'I'll help you up first.'

Margie glanced at the television and sees that the introduction to the film is about to end.

'No!' she almost shouts. 'I mean, get me a drink of water first, please.' She tried again to find the control but her arm wasn't long enough. She heard Annie returning so she crawled as fast as she could across the carpet on her hands and knees, hit the off button on the television and only made it back to lie beside the chair before Annie returned with the water. Annie helped Margie onto the chair and gave her the water.

'There you are. Take a big swallow, you'll feel better.'

'Thanks.' Margie took a sip of the water and handed the glass back to Annie.

'I think I better stay with you until your Maureen comes home. Or maybe I should call her… '

'Not at all, there's no need for that. Sure, it's only a touch of vertigo. I'll be grand in a minute or two. I'm grand, Annie, really.'

Annie turned to go but suddenly remembered, 'My head, I nearly forgot why I came. Are you going to Higs's funeral tomorrow?'

'Are you serious! I wouldn't miss it for a chance of wrecking the bed with George Clooney. I'm just thinking, Annie, the television cameras will be there too. I think I'll have an early night as I want to be well-rested. Tomorrow will be a long day.'

'Goodnight, then, Margie. I'll see you in the morning.'

''Night, Annie.' When Margie heard the front door close, she moved the chair back and picked up the control. She sank back into the chair and turned the television on. Her Rosary beads were still on the arm of the chair. She blessed herself with the beads. 'I'll make this up to you, Lord. I'll go off chocolate for Lent.' And Fifty Shades Of Grey began.

Maureen and Shantel walked along the streets engrossed in conversation. Shantel was wearing a pair of

Maureen's heels and her best pair of jeans. She looked much better in them than she did in the red miniskirt. They reached Murphy's Pub.

Maureen stopped to ask Shantel, 'How do I look?'

'We both look too good for this dump.' Shantel pushed the door open and they went in.

Duffy and Lecky drove along in the patrol car, stopping directly outside Murphy's Pub. Lecky was eating a double burger. He shoved the remainder of it into his mouth making his cheeks bulge so much he looked like a hamster.

'You missed a great night out last night. I couldn't believe the way Prindy encouraged me to go out. She never lets me go out.' He sneezed and sprayed ketchup over Moore's face. 'Sorry about that, here, let me wipe it for you.' He took a soiled hanky from his pocket and raised it to Duffy's face.

Duffy slapped his hand away. 'I'll do it myself.' He wiped his face with a paper tissue and threw it out of the window.

'I was really looking forward to a night out with you and the boys. But my piles were killing me.'

Duffy thought back to the night before when he and Prindy were in bed. They were canoodling under the blankets when, suddenly, the dog barked. Prindy's head popped up.

'What was that!'

'I didn't hear anything but I think your bazookas broke my eardrums.' The dog barked again. 'Now, where were we?' Prindy disappeared under the covers, giggling.

'I always suspected your husband was brain-damaged. Now, I'm wondering how he wasn't de-capitated.'

'Are you telling me you don't like it?'

'Oh, I love it.' Duffy was out of breath. 'It's just that, years ago, I developed this habit of breathing and I can't seem to break it.'

Prindy threw herself on top of Duffy and pulled the covers back over them. They rolled around on the bed in the throes of passion.

The bedroom door opened and Lecky walked in. He lookd at the moving covers for a few seconds, then took his coat off and hung it in the wardrobe. Next, he took off his shoes. Prindy, came up for air, saw her husband and froze.

'You're home!' She gave a nervous laugh. 'Why didn't you speak?' Duffy lay perfectly still as Prindy's right breast was poking his eye.

'I forgot my key. I was banging on the door but you didn't hear me. Anyway, I climbed in the window. I thought Rocky was going to attack me. You're sleeping early. The way you were rolling around there you must have been having a bad nightmare. It's a good thing I came home when I did or you might have done yourself an injury.'

'But... ' Prindy stammered. 'You went to the stag night.'

'Aye, it's still going strong, but sure it was no craic without Duffy. I should phone him and see if he's feeling any better. He has no one, only me. He'll be laying in that lonely flat, curled up in a freezing cold bed.' Lecky had the number dialled before Prindy could stop him.

Under the bedcovers, Duffy was sweating profusely. His mobile phone was in his trousers which were tangled around his ankles, ringing loudly.

'What's that?' Lecky was confused. 'That's the same ringtone as Duffy.'

Quick as a flash, Prindy said,. 'It's that bloody ice cream man again, at this time of night. Will you go and sort him out? Tell him you'll arrest him for disturbing the peace!'

Lecky reached for his shoes.

'Never mind your shoes!' Prindy shouted. 'Go on! Get him before he gets away!'

As soon as her husband was out of the room, Prindy flung the covers back. She put the soles of her feet against Duffy's back and pushed as hard as she could. Duffy flew out of the bed and hit the floor with a bang. He lay there gasping for air, drips of sweat rolling down his face.

'Dear God! I thought you were going to suffocate me!'

'Get your clothes, quick! Get in the wardrobe before he comes back!' She heard Lecky's footsteps coming back. 'For God's sake, move, will you!'

Prindy jumped out of bed, giving Duffy a hefty kick in the ribs. He staggered to the wardrobe. Prindy pushed him inside and threw his clothes in after him. Then, she raced across to the bed, jumping in just as Lecky opened the door.

'The bastard got away but I'll be laying in wait for him the next time. He'll not be flaunting his illegal ice cream on my street… I think I should try to phone Duffy again.'

'Never mind, Duffy,' Prindy snapped. 'Get into bed now!'

Lecky began to undress. He folded each item he removed and stacked them neatly on top of each other. Naked, he stood smiling at Prindy.

'Prindy, love, is there any chance of me getting a bit?'

'Didn't you get it at Christmas! Turn off the lights and go to sleep.'

Lecky climbed into into bed. Two seconds later, the sound of Prindy's hand slapping his face reverberated around the darkened room.

'You're nothing but an animal!'

'Sorry, Prindy, dear!' Five seconds later, Lecky was snoring loudly.

Prindy eased herself out of bed and went to the wardrobe. 'Come on,' she whispered.

Duffy tip-toed past the bed. Lecky suddenly stopped snoring. 'Duffy, you're a boyo,' Lecky laughed. Duffy froze. The snoring started again, louder than ever. Prindy opened the bedroom door very quietly and pushed Duffy out. He crept downstairs to the back door. But, just as he reached for the handle, the sound of growling comes from behind him. He turned around to see Rocky facing him, teeth bared. Duffy said very quietly,

'It's okay, Rocky boy, it's me.' Rocky advanced towards him, saliva dripping from his tongue. 'Good dog! Good dog!' Duffy swung around and grabbed the door handle but Rocky sprung into action, biting down hard on his bare arse.

'She was really annoyed at me for coming home early,' Lecky's voice brought Duffy back to the present.

'Well, you'll know the next time you're allowed out to stay out late,' Duffy advised. 'She'll be grateful to you for giving her the time to do the things she enjoys doing when you're not there.'

'Know something, Duffy? I can always listen to your advice. You're right, I'll let her do her own thing and maybe when I get home she'll do mine.'

Duffy shifted his behind trying to get the bite on his bum in a more comfortable position on the doughnut cushion.

'I didn't think you'd be at work tonight. You're feeling better then?' Lecky looked at the cushion under Duffy's behind. 'Why are you sitting on that cushion with the hole in the middle of it? Have you got piles?'

'Oh, aye, piles and piles of them.'

Soupy and Biddley came around the corner on their way to Murphy's Pub. Biddley tripped over something and fell to the ground. Soupy bent down to help her up. She managed to steady herself by holding on tightly to a lamp-post. Soupy encouraged her to let go of the lamp post.

But, when she did, instant dizziness forced her to break into a trot. Which ended at the next lamp-post where she knocks herself out.

'Look at that.' Duffy shakes his head. ''tis enough to put you off drink.' The patrol car drove away.

Chapter Ten

The pub was filled to capacity and everyone wanted a drink at the same time. Liam and his nephew, Conor, just back from university, struggled to keep up with the orders. Bosco was squashed tightly against the bar by a grossly overweight man, shouting his order at Liam.

'Will you serve this big fat B.' Bosco was breathless. 'Before he pushes my spine down my nose!'

'Why don't you get yourself behind the bar and give us a hand!'

'There's not a hope of getting me on that side of the bar. This is my night out to toast Higs. God rest him.'

The fat man threw himself on top of Bosco and shouted at Liam, 'Can I have a drink before I die!' Bosco's back was breaking.

'For God's sake, Liam, give him a drink, will you!'

'I'll give him a drink if you help us out for a few hours.'

'All right!' Bosco's face had turned purple. 'Just tell this elephant to get off me!' Liam served the man his drink. And he dislodged himself from Bosco.

'Come on! Get your coat off and get stuck in.' Liam threws him a plastic apron. 'Put that on, it'll keep you dry.'

'Right, who's next?' Bosco asked. A chorus of voices shouted orders at him. 'Shaddup! One at a time!'

Madge and Josie come into the pub and went to their usual table. But two men were sitting in their seats beside Corky. Madge was more than a little annoyed. She pushed her way through the crowd to the bar.

'Liam!' she shouted. 'I want my usual table and I can't get it because you let two strangers sit there!'

'I'm very busy, Madge… '

'If I don't get my seat, me and Josie will never set foot in here again. You'll not be so busy then!'

'Right.' Liam walked over to Corky and unceremoniously plucked him out of his wheelchair, sitting him on a stool, pushing the wheelchair out of the way. He had a quiet word with the two men. They nodded in agreement. Liam returned to Madge.

'Well?'

'The two men have agreed to sit on stools and give you both the chairs.'

'I should think so and all.' Madge was happy again.

Liam grabbed two stools from behind the bar and put them beside Corky for the two men. Madge took her seat beside them. Josie sat down, smiling broadly at the men.

'C'mere, are any of you two single? Because my friend here is available.'

'If you don't shut your mouth I'm going to pulverise you!' Madge's face was like thunder. The two men rose with their beers, moving quickly to stand by the window.

Maureen and Shantel managed to get a standing space beside the ladies toilet.

'Look at this place!' Shantel rolled her eyes. 'There's nothing in here that would even give you a bad thought.'

The karaoke started and the first ones up to sing were Soupy and Biddley. They murdered Sonny and Cher's, I Got You, Babe. A chorus of loud boos all but drowned them out. Maureen was facing the pub's main entrance. The door opened and the most gorgeous woman she had ever seen came in. She was just about to tell Shantel to turn round to look, when Barry followed closely behind, holding her hand. All eyes were on them, except Shantel who had her back to them.

'Oh, for God's sake.'

'What?' Shantel's eyes followed Maureen's gaze and she froze. 'Don't let him see that you're annoyed. Smile, girl, smile.'

'The bastard!' Shantel was livid. 'I can't even leave. He would see me and think I am annoyed. I knew I shouldn't have come here tonight!'

She stormed into the toilet, banging the door behind her and almost knocked Josie out, who was coming in behind her.

'Oh, sorry, Josie!'

'No worries, love.' Josie felt her nose. 'I've had harder knocks than that in my life.' She suddenly looked confused.

'Are you okay?'

'Do you know why I came in here, love?'

'Did you want to use the toilet?'

'Aye,' Josie smiled. 'How did you know that?'

'Lucky guess?'

Josie went into the toilet. Shantel took lipstick from her handbag and looked at herself in the mirror.

'Get a grip on yourself, girl.' She straightened her back, opened the toilet door and went back into the pub.

'Are you all right?' Maureen asked.

'No, but I will be when I get a drink.'

Maureen opened her purse and gave her a twenty-pound note. 'Here, get yourself a double.' Shantel pushed her way to the bar. Liam and Bosco were busy serving customers. She waited impatiently and, was just about to give up hope of ever being served, when Conor came out of the store room. He had been watching her since she arrived at the pub.

'What can I do for you?' He gave her a devastating smile; her knees wobbled.

'Um… Agh!' Shantel had lost her composure. 'Could I have… Can I have a double vodka and a Corps Light… please?'

'You… can have anything you want.' He looked at her intently. 'A double vodka coming up.' Connor gave her the two drinks. As he took the money, his hand brushed hers. For a second their eyes met. Shantel was still blushing when she went back to Maureen.

'Are you all right? You looked flushed.'

Shantel was breathless with excitement. 'I think I'm in love.' She looked across to the bar at Connor. Maureen followed her vision.

'What! Five minutes ago, Barry was the only one for you.'

'Barry who? Do you know who Connor is? I've never seen him before.'

The music started again and a very sexy voice started to sing, I Am A Woman In Love. It was Barry's date. She had a deep, husky voice. Her hips swayed provocatively to the rhythm of the music. Barry's friends wolf whistled and cheered her on. Barry jumped up, grabbing her waist, and they danced sensuously. He ran his hands down her back and over her hips. They kissed passionately to another round of cheers.

Shantel is completely unperturbed by the spectacle. 'Well? Do you know who Connor is?'

'Conor is Liam's nephew. I told you about him before.'

'You didn't tell me he was a babe.'

Madge and Josie were watching Barry and the woman gyrate around the tables.

Madge was disgusted. 'Look at that. They're practically tearing each other's clothes off!'

Josie wistfully said, 'Oh, the memories!'

'Oh, now you can remember what sex is?'

'I can, Madge… I just can't remember who I did it with.'

Soupy and Biddley were so drunk on the dance floor that they had to hold each other up. Biddley suddenly started to cry.

'What's wrong, pet?''

'Do you think I'm too old for my line of work, Soupy?'

'What are you talking about, wee girl? Sure, you're just reaching your prime.'

'You always were a gentleman, Soupy Campbell.'

'People might think I'm lonely on my own.' Biddley sniffed. 'I don't want to look desperate.'

'Maybe you and me should get married?' Soupy gave her a toothless grin.

'Jesus Christ! I'm not that desperate!'

Back at the bar, Bosco was trying to keep up with the orders. The clientele were getting drunker and louder and he was sweating so much that his shirt was stuck to his back. He shouted across at Liam,

'Hey! When do we get a break?'

'When we close!' Liam shouted back.

Maureen made her way to the bar to buy a drink. 'Hiya, love,' Bosco said. 'What can I get you?'

Liam saw Bosco talking to Maureen. He went over to serve her.

'I'll get this.' He smiled at Maureen. 'What can I get you?'

'The usual for me and Shantel, please.'

Are you enjoying yourself?' He gave Maureen the drinks. She tried to pay him. 'They're on the house.'

'Thank you, Liam. Aye, the craic's good? You must be exhausted.'

'Aye, I'm tired, but it's worth it. Higs got a good turn-out. The takings will go some way to help pay for his funeral. I like your hair like that. Listen, there's a good film showing. I was going to ask you if… '

'We need help here,' Bosco shouts. 'Any day now!'

'Sorry.' Liam walked away. Maureen made her way to Shantel.

Maureen took the drink back to Shantel. 'I'm going to kill my da tonight if my ma doesn't do it first.'

Chapter Eleven

The chapel was empty except for two elderly ladies who had stayed behind after mass to say the Rosary. Their heads were bowed as they prayed fervently before a statue of The Blessed Virgin. One of the women blessed herself with her Rosary beads. She got to her feet and genuflected to the altar, before walking up to Higs's coffin. The second woman blessed herself and went to join her friend. They peered into the coffin. The top half of Higs's head was covered with a thick bandage and he had two black eyes.

The first woman looked at the corpse. 'Where do you think he is now?'

The second woman replied, 'I'm in the house of God so I'm not going to be disrespectful… I hope he's burning in Hell with that man I was married to! Sorry, now, Lord!'

'We should say a prayer for him,' the first woman remarked.

'Aye, so we should.'

They abruptly turned on their heels and walked out of the chapel. The last remaining candle flickered and died. And Higs was left alone in the darkness.

Fifty Shades Of Grey had ended and Margie was left stunned. She stared at the blank television screen unable to believe what she had just seen.

'Margie girl… you don't know what sex is.' She looked at the thinning wedding ring on her finger. 'That bastard's idea of foreplay is, brace yourself!' She turned the television off and went upstairs to bed.

Meanwhile, in Murphy's Pub, the party for Higs was in full swing. Everyone was drunk, including Maureen and Shantel. Connor looked across at Shantel, again. She gave him a very suggestive wink.

'I think Liam is finally going to ask me out.'

'About time too. The four of us can double date. You and Liam and me and Conor.'

'When did Connor ask you out?'

'He didn't.' Shantel drained the remainder of her drink. 'What makes you think he's going to?'

'I wish I was as sure of getting into heaven.' Shantel smiled. 'C'mere, if I marry Connor and you marry Liam, you'll be my auntie.'

Bosco was practically running from customer to customer, trying to keep up with the orders.

'Hi, Liam. It is closing time?'

'You don't ask that when you're on the other side of the bar.' Liam shouted at the top of his voice, 'Last orders, ladies and gentlemen, please.'

There was a stampede to the bar and everyone wanted doubles. Olga was dancing around a pole in the middle of the small dance space. The men were whooping and egging her on. She played to the crowd and wrapped her leg around the pole, hugging it suggestively. Soupy and Biddley were dancing beside her, cheek-to-cheek. Soupy's back was to Olga as she swayed and wiggled her behind. He suddenly let go of Biddley and grabbed Olga's bum. Biddley fell to the floor with a thud. Olga turned around and punched Soupy on the nose. He fell beside Biddley, who was flat out on the floor.

'Soupy, pet, did that bitch hit you!' Biddley somehow managed to reach up and grab Olga's hair. It came off in her hand. All eyes were now on Olga's bald head. It was obvious to everyone that she was definitely a he. Frozen with shock, Barry stared at Olga in disbelief.

Madge shouted from the corner, 'Hey, Barry! Have you been putting somewhere you shouldn't?' Everyone roared with laughter, especially Shantel. Flushed with anger and embarrassment, Barry walked up to Olga, throwing a hard punch at her stomach. Olga didn't flinch. She eyeballed Barry for a few seconds then, in a flash, her fist shot up and hit him in the face with a punch so hard it sent him flying across the floor. He was out cold at Shantel's feet. She grabbed a half-full pint of beer from a table and poured it slowly over his face. He struggled to his feet, pulling himself up, until he was eye-level with Olga. There was another face off. Defeated, Barry stumbled out of the bar.

'Jesus!' Bosco relaxed. 'I'm glad I'm not on the dating scene anymore!'

The karaoke suddenly played the Rocky theme, all the men gathered around Olga, congratulating her and slapping her on the back.

It was the morning after the party. The pub was dark and deathly silent. Liam was asleep on a bench. Bosco was hanging on a coat hook behind the bar. Soupy was sprawled on the floor, with an arm around Olga. The silence was broken by a loud knocking on the front door. Liam stirred, disoriented for a few seconds. Another, even louder series of knocks.

'Whoever you are,' Liam shouted, 'I'm going to make mince out of you!' He tried to stand up but immediately trips over Olga. Swearing, he kicked her in the ribs. He held onto the bar for a second to steady himself. His head felt like there was a hammer inside pounding a rumba on his skull. He went to the door and looked through the small stained-glass window. To his horror, he saw Detective McKnight pacing back and forth in front of the pub. He rushed over to Soupy and shouted in his ear, 'Get up, now!'

'I didn't do it, constable, there's my hand to God.' He opened his eyes. 'Oh, it's yourself, Liam. I thought you were the police.'

'They're at the door.' Liam ran his hands through his hair. 'Wake yer woman… I mean, yer man up, now!' He slaps Bosco's face, hard. 'Wake up. It's the police! What time is it?' He looked at the clock on the wall behind the bar but it had stopped. 'Dear God, the bastards are going to fine me for after-hours drinking!'

When Bosco heard the word police, he pole-vaulted into action. 'The police! I knew it. They're coming to get me.' Bosco ran to the back of the pub. 'I need to get out of here!' He ran to the toilet, followed by Soupy.

Olga was having trouble waking up. There was another loud series of knocks. Liam shouted at Olga, "Get up!" But she just moaned and turned over on her other side. In desperation, Liam grabbed her coat, yanking her off the floor and threw her into a chair. Before he could decide what to do with her, there was another loud series of knocks, followed by the angry voice of McKnight, demanding to be let inside. Liam opened the door.

'You took your time.' The Detective looked around the bar.

'Sorry… um, I was in the toilet. Wonky stomach.' McKnight was staring at Olga's bald head. His eyes fell to her mini-skirt. At that moment, Olga opened her eyes and gave him a very slow, suggestive wink. And, in her deep guttural voice, said,

'Well, hello there, big boy.'

Detective McKnight looked at Liam, one eyebrow raised.

'Come on, now, didn't I tell you hours ago to go home?' Liam took hold of Olga's arm and shoved her out the door.

'Foreigners!' Liam shrugged his shoulders. 'What can I do for you, Detective McKnight?'

'You can tell me the truth.'

'The truth? Of course.' Liam took a cautious breath. 'The truth about what?'

'I have reason to believe that a crime was committed by a person or persons who frequent this establishment!' The Detective swung on his heels. 'And, it is my duty to inform you that, if you know anything about this matter, it would be advisable for you to come clean. Now!'

'Come clean about what?' Liam tried to remember if anything happened at the party last night, but his mind was a blank. 'I don't know what you are talking about.'

The Detective gave Liam a penetrating stare. 'Oh, did I forget to mention the nature of the crime? There's been a kidnapping.'

'A kidnapping?' Liam was completely thrown. 'But... what do you mean, a kidnapping. I don't understand.'

'You don't understand what a kidnapping is?

'Well, of course, I know what a kidnapping is. But, this is Tullamoragh. No one gets kidnapped here. Look, my clientele might be a bit... are a bit mad, but they would never knowingly hurt a living being!'

'Ah, well, there you are, you see. The kidnap-ee was already dead.'

'Eh?'

'Sometime between ten p.m. last night and seven a.m. this morning,' McKnight's eyes never left Liam's. 'Cornelius Henry Hegarty's body disappeared from the Catholic chapel.

'Holy Mother of God!' Soupy staggered out of the toilet. 'Somebody stole Higs? Is he on a run of bad luck or what? First, murdered, then, kidnapped! Still, on the plus side, it'll save his Mrs funeral expenses.'

The Detective looked at his watch.

'Soupy just called in to do a bet for me on the two o'clock race at Newmarket.' Liam threw Soupy a threatening look. 'Isn't that right, Soupy?'

'I think you'll find you're a bit late. It is two o'clock now.'

'In the afternoon?' Liam was confused. 'And it's Tuesday? Right?'

When Bosco heard this, he came rushing out of the toilet. 'I'll have a double brandy, Liam.'

'And I'll have a Guinness.' Soupy licked his lips. 'And Bosco is paying for it.'

Liam poured the two drinks. 'Bosco, did you hear what the Detective said? Higs is missing from the chapel. Someone actually stole him! It's unbelievable. How could that happen? A coffin is very heavy. It must have taken a few people to carry it.'

'They didn't bother with the coffin,' the Detective replied. 'They just took the body.'

'My God, that's disgusting! Imagine lifting a dead body from its coffin!' Liam shivered at the thought. 'Is nothing sacred anymore!'

Madge and Josie come into the pub. Josie saw Detective McKnight. 'Look, Madge, there's a strange man.'

'I see him. I'm not blind, you know!'

'That's all for now!' The Detective walked to the door. 'But we'll be keeping a very close eye on these premises.' He left. Madge took a hankie from her handbag and bent over to wipe a chair before she sat on it.

"Hi, Madge,' Soupy remarked. 'You have some arse on you.' Quick as a flash, Madge turned around and hit him with her handbag.

'All right. That's enough!' Liam took Soupy by the arm. 'C'mon, out you go.'

Soupy shouted from outside, 'Is it all right if I come back later?'

'Dear God! Someday I'm going to kill him.' Liam was at the end of his tether. 'Madge, I need to pee.' Josie was jumping up and down.

'Well, go to the toilet then. And, remember, pull everything down and then pull them all back up again. No, wait a minute, I'll go with you. I want no flash floods in here today. Liam put up two drinks.' Madge takes Josie into the ladies room.

'My head is bursting,' Bosco groaned. 'You shouldn't have let me drink so much last night. I can't remember anything.'

'No one poured the drink down your neck.' Liam turned off the lights and walked over to open the curtains. The door burst open and Soupy came rushing in.

'Liam! Liam! I remember something!'

"Get out, before Madge comes back or she'll make mince meat out of you!' Soupy was very agitated.

'But, Liam, I know where…'

Liam pulled the curtains open and jumped two feet into the air, backwards. 'Holy Mother of God!'

Soupy continued, '… Higs is.'

The blood drained from Liam's face.

Bosco dropped his glass on the floor. 'Am I awake?'

Chapter Twelve

Higs was sitting bolt upright at a table, one of his legs was resting on another chair. Liam and Bosco stared at him open-mouthed, horrified at the sight in front of them.

'How did he get here?' Liam looked at Soupy. 'How did you know he was here?'

'That's what I was trying to tell you. We stole Higs from the chapel and brought him here.' Liam held his breath.

'Who is we?'

'Bosco and me and you!'

'Oh, my God! Oh, my God!' Liam tried to remember anything about the night before. The sound of the toilet flushing pole-vaulted him into action. He hurriedly closed the curtains and picked up Bosco's broken glass from the floor just as Madge and Josie come out of the ladies room.

'Are you all right, Liam? You look like you've seen a ghost. It's very dark in here, I'll open the curtains.' Madge moved towards the window.

'Don't touch them curtains!' Liam shouted.

'Calm your hormones,' Madge shouted back just as loud. 'It's broad daylight out there, you know.'

'We're closed.'

'Closed? What are you talking about?' Madge snapped. 'It's quarter-past-two in the afternoon.'

'There's an electrical fault.' Liam thought on his feet. 'It's too dangerous for you to be here… There could be a fire!'

'What are you talking about?' Josie wagged her finger at Liam. 'Me and Madge were in three pubs in Derry when they were blown up and we only suffered minor cuts and bruises. We're not afraid of a wee fire!'

'Look,' Liam ushered them to the door. 'You need to go now!'

'Get your hands off me, this minute.' Madge tried to pull her arm away from Liam's grasp. Liam opened the door, pushed them outside and banged the door shut.

Madge kicked the door a couple of times and Josie hit it with her handbag.

'How dare you push me!' Madge roared at the top of her voice. 'You dying-looking bastard!' The three men stood mutely staring at the closed curtains. Liam went behind the bar and drank whiskey from a bottle.

'I thought you were never going to drink again?'

'This could all be a bad dream.'

'So it could,' Bosco agreed.

'Soupy, go over and see if he's still there.' Liam was rigid with tension. 'And I'll give you a drink.'

Soupy walked gingerly towards the curtains and stopped. 'Will you make it a double?' Liam nodded. Soupy peeked behind the curtains. 'Nope, he's still there.'

'We're in deep trouble.' Liam paced back and forth. 'How did we get into the chapel? The doors must be a foot thick.' Liam had a sudden flashback.

He was inside the darkened chapel. Higs was thrown over his shoulder and he was standing on a pew, with one knee on the window sill, struggling to lift the heavy corpse up to the level of the open window. Bosco and Soupy were on the outside of the chapel waiting beneath the window.

Bosco whispered very loudly, 'Liam, don't throw Higs out till Soupy gets on my shoulders'. Bosco got down on his knees to let Soupy climb up. But they were both very drunk and immediately lost their balance. They tried again but, this time, Soupy fell backwards into a rose bush.

'I think I got a thorn in my arse!' Soupy lay in the bush moaning. Bosco reached down and dragged him to his feet.

'Look, Soupy, when you get up on my shoulders, this time, you'd better stay there. All you have to do is reach up and catch Higs when he comes out.'

Liam shouted, 'What the hell is going on out there? At this rate, it will be daylight before we get him out! Hurry up!'

'We'll be sorted in a minute. Right, Soupy, you're going to stand on top of my shoulders and, remember, this time, don't fall off.'

'Right,' Soupy repeated, 'Don't fall off.' He managed to stay on for a few seconds, long enough for Liam to see his silhouette through the stained-glass window.

'Are you ready, Soupy? Right, here he comes.' With one almighty heave, Liam pushed Higs out of the window, but the buckle of Higs's belt caught on the window latch and the body was left dangling half-in and half-out of the window.

Soupy grabbed hold of Higs, pulling his arms as hard as he could. 'He's stuck. I can't move him.'

'My back is going to break any minute.' Bosco was purple in the face. 'Pull him harder!'

Liam stood on his tip-toes and wrestled the belt away from the latch. 'Pull him now!'

At that moment, Soupy made the mistake of looking up into Higs's pasty-grey face. 'Sacred Heart of God!' He let go of the corpse and they both fell backwards. Two seconds later, Higs hit the ground. Always seeing the positive in any negative, Soupy looked over at Higs's crumpled frame on the grass and remarked,

'Isn't it a good thing he's already dead? For if he fell like that when he was living, sure the fall would have only killed him.'

The full realisation of what they had done hit Liam. 'Oh, my God!' Liam shouted. 'Oh, my God! What have we done!'

'I hope we didn't break one of them stained-glass windows,' Bosco lamented. 'We could be in a lot of bother.'

'We are in a lot of bother. We stole a fucking dead body!'

Soupy remarked, 'Well, sure, didn't no one else want it!'

'I don't know about you,' Bosco pointed out. 'But I couldn't carry a dead body all the way from the chapel to the pub. Then, Bosco had a flashback.

Higs was going at speed down the hill from the chapel and he seemed to be on wheels.

'I know how we got Higs here!' Bosco hurried into the store room and came back pushing Corky's wheelchair. 'We brought him here in this.'

'But, what happened to Corky! Jesus! Did we dump him somewhere? This is a living nightmare.' Liam looked at the closed curtains. 'We need to get rid of Higs now!'

'How?' Bosco asked. 'It's broad daylight out there.'

'We could put sunglasses on him,' Soupy suggested. 'Stick a fag in his mouth and push him in the wheelchair.'

'Push him where?' Liam asked.

Soupy thought for a few seconds. 'I know! We'll take him to Biddley's house. Sure, it's only around the corner. She'll be out at this time of the day. That's what we'll do. We'll take him there and throw him in her bed.'

'And what do you think Biddle will do when she comes home and finds a corpse in her bed?'

'She won't even realise he's deceased. She always says most of her clients are dead if they only had the wit to stiffen.'

'Right. Biddley's it is.' Liam looked at his watch. 'We'll take him now. We'll go back later after the pub closes tonight and take him back to the chapel.

'We'll have to break in again.' Bosco started to sweat thinking about it. 'Do you not think that would be pushing our luck?'

'We'll park beside the Grotto outside, someone is bound to find him there. C'mon, Bosco, let's get him into the wheelchair.'

Liam and Bosco got hold of Higs, carefully manoeuvring him into the wheelchair. But the one leg that had been resting on the chair was sticking straight out in front of him.

'Don't just stand there, Soupy,' Liam snapped. 'Lend us a hand.'

'Well, now, Liam, I'm feeling a bit weak at the moment. I might be fit to help if I had a drop of whiskey to hydrate me.'

'Pour yourself a whiskey. Hurry up!'

Soupy poured himself a very large whiskey and threw it back. 'Right, what do you want me to do?'

'Come over here and push his leg down.' Soupy hesitated.

'Oh, I'm not sure about that.'

'Just do it!'

Soupy walked over to the wheelchair. Closing his eyes, he put his hand on Higs's leg and pushes it down with all his might. But Rigor Mortis had long since set in and, as the leg went down, Higs shot forward, head-butting Soupy. Soupy's eyes flew open, staring into Higs's face. He let go of the leg. Higs fell back into the wheelchair with a thud.

'Mother of God!' Soupy was chalk-white.

Bosco said, 'He's as stiff as a board.'

Soupy remarked, 'It's Biddley's lucky day.'

'If he wasn't dead, I'd kill him.' Liam went behind the bar to get some rope. He tied it around Higs's ankle and threw the other end of the rope under the wheelchair. 'Right. I'll pull on his ankle from behind the chair. Bosco, you hold on to his shoulders. Don't let go until his leg is down.' Bosco took his position behind Higs, holding him tightly. Liam pulled the rope as hard as he could. But all it did was force Higs out of the chair into a half-standing, half-bending position.

'All his life his arse was sore sitting.' Bosco took a sip of water. 'Now that he's dead, he wants to stand up. His wife always said he was contrary bastard.'

Liam said, 'He's going to sit on that chair if I have to throw Soupy on top of him!'

'Are you mad!' Soupy shouted. 'There's not a hope in hell of me getting into that chair with him! I wouldn't do it for all the money in the Credit Union or the Bank Of Ireland. Or all the banks in Ireland!'

'I'll give you a bottle of whiskey.'

'Right. Where do you want me to sit?' Soupy rubbed his hands together at the thought of a whole bottle of whiskey.

'Turn your back to him, then sit on his leg until it's down.'

Soupy said, 'Bottle of whiskey first!'

Liam went behind the bar for the whiskey. Soupy quickly shoved the bottle into his pocket. He walked hesitantly across the floor, stopping dead in front of the wheelchair.

'For God's sake!' Liam shouted. 'Will you just do it!'

Soupy gave Higs a nervous sideways glance and threw his leg over Higs's leg. He sat down but, instantly, pole-vaulted out of the chair.

'Jesus, Mary and Joseph! The dirty minger! His leg isn't the only organ that's standing to attention!' Soupy rubbed his bum.

'His leg is down. Thank, God.' Liam had, no sooner spoken when the leg shot back out again. The three men looked at it in disbelief.

Bosco said, 'Well, that didn't work.'

'Bosco, lock the door.' Liam got sunglasses and a cap someone left behind in the pub and put them on Higs. 'You'd nearly think he is alive. Okay, I'll push the chair, Soupy, you walk in front of him, hopefully, no one will notice his leg. Bosco, keep your eyes open for any hazards.'

Bosco said, 'I need to go to the toilet first.'

'Me too!' Soupy followed him. 'Isn't it funny how whiskey doesn't linger long in my system?'

Liam remarked drily, 'Arsenic couldn't linger long in your system.'

Liam tried one more time to bend the leg but no luck. Bosco and Soupy hurried back from the toilet. The three of them took their designated positions around the wheelchair. That's when the door flew open with a bang and Biddley fell in backwards. She lay there, sprawled on the dirty floor. Too drunk to recognise any of the men, all she saw were four potential clients.

'C'mon, you boyos, it's your lucky day. I have a special on today, buy one, get one free. But you'll need to hurry because the offer ends at… What time is it?'

Soupy smiles broadly. 'Hello, Biddley, pet.'

''Tis yourself, Soupy? Sure there's no charge to you. And yer good-looking man in the wheelchair there can take as long as he likes.'

'Well, that's good, for it might take a while to warm him up,' Soupy winked at Liam. 'Why don't we take him to your house and you can sort him out there?'

'Suits me,' Biddley responds. 'But I don't like standing up. I feel safer when I'm horizontal.'

Liam replied, 'You don't need to stand up, Biddley. C'mon, fellas, we'll put her on her client's lap. Would you like that, Biddley?'

'Ah, sure that's a grand idea altogether!'

Liam and Bosco lifted Biddley off the floor and sat her on her Higs's lap. 'How is that?' Liam asked. Biddley had a great big smile on her face. '

I'll tell you what, sir, we have a live one here!'

'Bosco, take a quick look outside to be on the safe side. Soupy, remember what I told you, stay in front of Higs.'

'There's just a couple of people on the other side of the street.' Looking at Higs. 'He looks like he's going on his holidays.'

'All right, Soupy, out you go.' Liam pushed the wheelchair out to the street with Soupy walking slightly ahead of him. Bosco was to the side of the wheelchair. Liam began to think that this might actually work, he relaxed a little. As they made their way along the street, Detective McKnight suddenly rounded a corner, heading in their direction. Liam quickly swung the wheelchair around, back in the pub's direction. Bosco hadn't seen the Detective so he shouted,

'Hi, Liam, where are you going!'

'C'mon, quick! Get Soupy. Hurry up!' He turned around, almost knocking Bosco down. 'It's the bastardin' police! Run!' The two of them caught up with Liam at the pub. They all tried to get into the pub at the same time and end up in a scrum at the door.

'Jesus!' Liam shouted. 'One at a time!' Bosco pushed Soupy out of the way. Liam ran with the wheelchair, hiding it behind the curtains but he turned the chair too quickly and Biddley fell off Higs's lap, landing heavily on the floor.

'Lock the door!' Liam looked down at Biddley.

'I thought we were going to my house? Not that, mind you, I can't do the deed just as well here. Just form a queue.' She rubs Higs's blue fingers. 'I'll do yer man here first.'

'Biddley, look at me!' Liam had a hold of Biddley's cheeks. 'The police might come in here. Do not make a sound or we'll all end up in jail. Do you hear me?'

Biddley pulled an imaginary zip across her lips. Liam pulled the curtains closed and went behind the bar. Detective McKnight started knocking loudly on the door. Liam checked that nothing was showing under the curtains. Soupy suddenly felt afraid.

'Maybe I should hide?'

'Stay where you are and keep your mouth shut.'

Liam had a quick look around the bar and decided that everything looked normal. 'Okay. Let the bastard in.'

'Why is the bar still closed?' McKnight asked.

Quick as a flash, Liam replied, 'We're doing some stock-taking. Can I get you a drink?'

'I hope you're not trying to encourage me to drink on duty.'

'Not at all… I meant tea or coffee.'

'I think I'll have to go home for a sleep.' Soupy walked to the door backwards. 'I'm knackered. I'm not fit for lifting a dead-weight like… ' Suddenly realising what he was saying, he stopped mid-sentence. The blood drained from Liam's face.

'Go on.' McKnight waited. 'You're not fit for lifting a dead-weight like… what?'

'Ah… um… like Biddley's knockers.'

Biddley hears Soupy. 'I heard that, Soupy Campbell! You had no bother lifting my knockers last night. You wee prevert!'

Liam went over to the closed curtains and pulled Biddley out by her arms. 'Did I not tell you to go home?'

'Aye, you did, but then you brought me back here again.' Biddley stared intently at Detective McKnight. Then the penny dropped. 'It's you! Where's your mask?'

The Detective shuffled uncomfortably from foot to foot. 'We've never met. I think you must be mistaking me for someone else.'

'I might forget a face. But I never forget an arse.'

Liam took hold of Biddley's arm and ushered her to the door. 'You need to go home now, we have work to do. Soupy, go with her and make sure she gets home safely. And, come straight back… for the stock-taking.'

Biddley was at the door, but she had one more thing to say to Detective McKnight, 'Anytime you feel like playing Batman again.' She gave him a suggestive wink. 'I'm your Robin.'

And she was gone. Bosco and Liam stared at McKnight. He wipes away a bead of sweat running down his temple.

'Look. I did not have sexual relations with that woman!'

'Oh, well, of course,' Liam agreed. 'That goes without saying.'

'Aye, so it does.' Bosco tried not to smirk. 'Goes without saying, so it does.'

'Right. Okay. We have it from a reliable source that three men with a wheelchair were seen loitering outside these premises at three o'clock this morning. Do either of you know anything about this?'

'Definitely not!' I was in bed at three o'clock this morning.'

'And do you have anyone who can verify your story?'

'I have. Bosco was with me, weren't you, Bosco?'

McKnight took out his notebook and began to write. 'So you were in bed, together.'

'No! We didn't sleep together. Bosco was on the sofa.'

'That's right,' Bosco reiterated.

McKnight put his notebook away and looked at both men, one eyebrow raised. 'So, you know nothing?'

'Not a thing!'

'That's right,' Liam emphasised. 'We know nothing.'

'I find that very hard to believe.' McKnight turned to walk away but stopped suddenly. 'Just to let you know, if I find out that you're lying to me, I will make personally sure that you are both locked up for the next ten years.' He turned on his heel and left.

'Jesus!' Bosco felt sick. 'What are we going to do with Higs?'

'If we can't get him back to the chapel, we'll have to bury him in a very deep hole!' Liam poured two drinks. 'Where the hell is Soupy? This is all his fault. If he hadn't brought that potcheen last night, we wouldn't have gotten pissed and Higs would still be in the chapel.'

Chapter Thirteen

Soupy came out of the bookies and bumped straight into Madge and Josie.

'How're you, Soupy? You look a bit red in the face.' Josie felt his head 'Are you okay?'

'Of course, he's okay, isn't he pickled in alcohol?' Madge said with her usual friendly venom. 'You tell that Liam fella that we'll be coming to the pub shortly and, if he doesn't let us in, we'll break his windows.' Madge stormed off.

'Tell Liam I'm not going to break his windows but I might have to hit him with my handbag or Madge will be very annoyed.' Josie shuffled off after Madge.

Soupy returned to the pub, flushed with excitement. He couldn't wait to give Liam the news.

'What kept you!' Liam was in a foul mood.

'Well, you see, I called into the bookies to do a wee bet... '

'You took time to go into the bookies when you know Higs is still here!' Liam grabbed Soupy by the neck.

Bosco jumped in between Soupy and Liam. 'For God's sake, if you kill him, we'll have two bodies to get rid of.'

Liam let go of Soupy and he fell to the floor, coughing. 'But, Liam, I have something to tell you!'

'Just tell him, Soupy, before he knocks you into the middle of next week.'

'The accumulators you and Higs did on Saturday came in.' Soupy was beside himself with excitement. 'You won on every race!'

'My God! We made a fortune… I made a fortune! Did you tell anyone about this?'

'I did not, Liam. I came straight here to tell you.'

'If you so much as breathe a word of this to anyone and that means Biddley too, I'll kill you.'

'How much did you win?' Bosco couldn't believe it.

'Fifty thousand, five hundred-and-twenty- seven-pounds… I can buy the pub.' Liam grabbed a bottle of whiskey and poured three drinks. He raised his glass. 'To Higs!'

'God rest his soul.' Soupy licked his lips and swallowed the whiskey.

'Amen to that!' Bosco emptied his glass.

'Soupy, give me the bookies slip.'

'The bookies slip? Well, you see… '

Madge's voice can clearly be heard shouting a greeting to someone outside.

Liam is instantly on alert. 'Quick! Get Higs out from behind the curtains and put him at that table in the corner.' Bosco pushed Higs into the corner table while Soupy lit a fag and shoved it in Higs's mouth. Liam rushed into the storeroom, coming back with a short black wig. He slapped the wig on Higs's head and went behind the bar as Madge and Josie came in. Madge threw him a defiant look, daring him to challenge her.

'Right, ladies, the usual?'

Margie and Cassie walked into the chapel for the funeral mass but the chapel was totally empty. Margie looked around her.

'There's no one here.'

Cassie walked up to the coffin to have one last look at Higs. 'Higs isn't here either!'

'What?' Margie went to the coffin. 'He's not here! What the…'. She almost swore. 'What's going on here?'

'I don't know. Do you think that they already buried him?'

'Without his coffin!' Margie tried to be nice. 'I know he was a total waster of a man but he still deserves a decent funeral.'

Father Divine walked onto the altar carrying fresh flowers. As soon as he saw Margie and Cassie, he did an about-face. But they saw him.

Margie calls after him. 'Father Divine.'

The Priest turned around to face them. 'Please keep your voice down.'

'Sorry, Father.' Margie took a step closer. 'We came for Higs's funeral mass, and he's not here. Where is he?'

'At this moment in time, I can't tell you that.' Father Divine walked swiftly to the door and exited. Margie and Cassie stared after him.

Father Divine hurried into the parochial house and phoned Sergeant Doherty. 'Hello? Is that you, Sergeant Doherty? Did you find the body yet?' He listened to the excuses the Sergeant makes.

'Well, you need to look harder. If it gets out that he was stolen from the chapel, I'll be expected to take security on and the Sunday collection doesn't run to that!' He slammed down the receiver and poured himself a double brandy.

Margie and Cassie come out of the chapel blessing themselves with holy water.

'There's something very strange going on here.' Margie folded her arms. 'Where the hell is Higs?'

'Well, I can tell you where he's not, in Murphy's Pub.'

Liam and Bosco were behind the bar nervously watching Josie deep in conversation with Higs. Soupy came out of the toilet and tried to coax her away but she was having none of it.

She carried on her conversation with Higs! 'You know, you remind me of my late husband. He was very good-looking too... or maybe I'm thinking of the coal man. Anyway, my husband wasn't like you in nature. He never listened to a word I said. As soon as I would start to talk he would put on his coat and go to the pub. You've sat there listening to every word I said. Would you like a wee drink?'

Madge was watching Josie's one-sided conversation and she was irritated. 'Josie, come back here this second!

He doesn't want to talk to you. Hey, Liam, I heard that Higs has absconded from the chapel.' Liam dropped the glass he was drying.

'Naw, I didn't hear that.' He tried to sound normal. He knew if Madge knew Higs was sitting a few feet from her, world war three would break out. Josie patted Higs's arm.

'I'll come back and talk to you when Madge gets drunk.'

Liam was afraid to take his eyes off Josie. 'This is going to end badly, Bosco!'

'It is.'

'We need to keep our wits about us.'

'Aye, stay calm.'

Liam pulled Soupy to one side. 'Give me the bookie slip. I'll want to get the money today.'

'I haven't got it.'

'What do you mean, you haven't got it? Where is it?'

'That's what I was going to tell you when Madge came in and threw us all into a panic. I gave it to Higs on Saturday night.'

'You what!' Liam's voice carried around the pub. Josie was startled, she jumped, spilling her drink on Madge.

'Mother of God!' Madge waved her fist at Liam. 'It's a good thing I don't have a dicky ticker. Look at my coat. It's soaked!'

'Sorry about that, Madge. Bosco, get Madge and Josie another drink.'

'Make mine a double, you owe me that. I'll have to pay to get this coat dry-cleaned.'

Liam pushed Soupy into the store room. 'Why would you give the slip to Higs? He was pissed out of his mind.'

'Higs asked me for it. He said he wanted to hide it where his wife couldn't find it. I laughed because everyone knew his accumulators never win.'

'You couldn't beat my luck! That's it then, the pub is gone.'

'I'm sorry,' Soupy apologised. 'So, I am.'

Liam comes out of the storeroom with a face like thunder. He became more agitated when he saw Josie back in conversation with Higs, giggling like a schoolgirl.

Liam went behind the bar and poured himself a treble whiskey. 'What's happened now?' Bosco couldn't take any more drama.

'Oh, you mean, apart from the dead body in the pub and the fact that I lost over fifty thousand pounds!'

'You what?'

Josie came to the bar humming a tune. 'Liam, I just want to buy yer man a wee drink to see if it will loosen him up a bit. Looking at the paleness of his skin I'd say he's a whiskey drinker.'

'I heard him saying he has somewhere to go.' Liam elbowed Soupy. 'Isn't that right, Soupy?'

'Indeed it is. Um… he wants me to take him to the doctor. He's suffering from constipation.'

Madge shouted across, 'I'm not surprised. He hasn't moved a muscle since we came in here.' Liam winked at Soupy. 'Now might be a good time to go?'

Soupy took hold of the wheelchair, pushing it to the door. 'But, Liam, what am I going to do with him?'

'It's getting dark out there. Leave him in some alleyway, away from the street.'

'Right, an alleyway off the road. I can do that.' Soupy pushed the wheelchair over the doorstep onto the street.

'If you mess this up, we'll all be jailed,' Liam emphasised. 'And you won't get a drink for the next ten years!'

'Don't worry now, Liam. I'll be sure to put him where he won't be noticed.'

Soupy pushed Higs out to the street. Liam watched him pushing the wheelchair, half with relief, half with trepidation. Soupy had no idea where he was going, but continued to walk anyway. He turned into the first alleyway he came to and parked Higs at the back door of a pool hall. He was about to walk away when a group of youths exited the hall. The first one out, fell over Higs. His friends fell about laughing.

Soupy apologised profusely, 'Sorry, son, sorry about the now! I'll just push him out of your way.'

'No worries,' one of the youths called. 'Sure, you're grand.'

The group walked out of the alleyway. Soupy pulled the blanket up tighter around Higs's neck. 'Don't worry yourself now, Higs. I know where you'll be as safe as a row of houses.' He was pushing the chair to the end of the alleyway, when he was suddenly hit in the face with a ten-pound note. He couldn't believe his luck! He examined the note carefully, before stuffing it into his pocket and hurried to the street before the owner of the money realised it was missing and came back looking for it. He was passing Sullivan's Pub when Biddley stepped out in front of him.

'Soupy, pet! I was on my way to Murphy's.'

She looked at Higs. 'I see yer man is still sleeping. That's the sign of a clear conscience or no conscience at all! Where are you two going? I'll come with you… '

Soupy was thrown into a panic. 'No, no! No need for that! I'll tell you what, we'll go back into Sullivans and I'll buy you a drink. I recently came into some unexpected money.'

'Happy days!'

'You go on in and order us a drink.' When she was safely inside, he had a comforting word with Higs. 'Right, Higs, I'm going to have one drink and I'll be straight back to sort you. Now, that's a promise!' Soupy went into the pub, leaving Higs at the mercy of any gangster that might come along.

Chapter Fourteen

Margie was sitting at the kitchen table drinking a cup of tea when Maureen came home. Her dinner was ready on the table prepared on a plate covered with cling film.

'Where's my da's dinner?'

'In the bin when I get my hands on him! He didn't come home last night.'

'He was still in the pub when Connor left me and Shantel home last night.'

'Who's Connor?'

'|According to Shantel, he's her future husband. You don't need to worry about my da staying at the pub anymore. Liam is closing it down tonight.'

'He's closing the pub down?' Margie was stunned. 'Why? What's happened?'

'Don't know. Don't care.' Maureen heated her dinner in the microwave and walked to the kitchen door.

'Where are you going? Sit down and eat your dinner at the table like a Christian.'

'I'll eat it while I'm getting ready.' She winked at her mother. 'I have a heavy date tonight.' She walked out of the kitchen with Margie calling after her,

'If you come across your father, tell him I went to a solicitor about getting a divorce.'

Three drunk men come out of Sullivan's Pub. The first man tripped over the wheelchair, knocking the wig off Higs's bald head. He picked the wig up from the ground and slapped it on back-to-front.

'Sorry, now. I hope I didn't incapacitate you?'

The second drunk sniggered. 'He's in a bloody wheelchair. He's already incompas... incompart... hammered!'

The third drunk took hold of the handles. 'He looks like he might be lost. C'mon, we'll give him a push.'

'Right, you are.' Drunk number three grabs the wheelchair. 'I'll push him.' He tried to push the chair but it won't budge.

'Get out of the way.' Drunk two intervenes. 'I'll do it.' None of them realised that the brake was on the chair.

Drunk two had one more go at pushing the wheelchair but it wouldn't budge. 'This thing is going nowhere!' He bent down and asked Higs, 'Where are you going, sir?' They waited for an answer.

Drunk three said, 'That's it then, he's on his own.' Drunks one and three start to walk away.

Drunk two persists, 'We can't just go and leave him here. He'll freeze to death!'

Customers were starting to gather in Murphy's Pub. Josie was in her usual seat. Madge came back from the bar with two drinks.

'I have the bloody heartburn again. I knew I shouldn't have eaten that stew.' She picked up her handbag. 'I'll have to go to the shop to get some Rennies, I'm not a bit well.'

'You don't look a bit well, Madge. I'll go to the shop and get them for you.'

'Will you remember the way back here?'

'Sure, it's only next door. I'll be back before you know it.'

Liam couldn't understand why there were so many people in the pub on a Tuesday night. Bosco was in his usual seat. Maureen strolled in and perched on a stool in front of Liam.

'Out on a Tuesday night?' Liam gave her a warm smile.

'I know you're closing down tonight.'

'So, that's why everyone is here,' Liam sighed. 'I was hoping to make a quick getaway.'

Liam poured a drink for Maureen. She took a sip. 'What will you do with yourself when you don't have to work nights in the pub anymore?'

"Let me think… I could take you to the cinema?'

'You'll have to ask me nicely.'

'Well, will you go to… ' Liam doesn't get to finish his sentence.

'Yes!

Shantel and Connor walked in and sat beside Maureen. Shantel gave Maureen a knowing wink. In the corner, Madge was becoming irritated because Josie has not returned with the Rennies.

'Liam, is that clock right?'

'It's ten minutes slow, Madge.'

'She's been gone an hour. I knew I shouldn't have let her go to the shop on her own!' Madge decided to go out and look for Josie. She shouted to Liam, 'I'll be back, don't touch my drink!' Madge was about to leave when the door opened and Josie came in backwards, pulling something.

'Madge, you'll never guess who I found?' She pulls Higs in. 'It's yer man, he was sitting outside Sullivan's Pub. He's blue with the cold. Soupy was nowhere about so I brought him back here to get heat.'

Liam is beside Josie in three giant steps. 'I'll take care of him now, Josie. You shouldn't be pulling that, it's too heavy for you.' Liam pushed the wheelchair over to where Bosco was. 'I'm going to kill Soupy!'

'You took your bloody time.' Madge was irate. 'What kept you? I could have been dead, waiting for you!'

'I had to push yer man and he's no featherweight, you know.'

Bosco pushed the wheelchair to the far side of the pub. Liam followed him and goes into a rant.

'Put him out of the way, I said. Where no one will see him I said. So, he leaves a dead body outside a pub! A pub!'

'Jesus!' Bosco was incredulous. 'He went on a pub crawl, with a corpse!'

'We can't even hide him now. I need to get the pub closed soon.

Liam hurried back behind the bar.

'Hi, Da, when are you intending to go home, because you're in big trouble?' Maureen waved her fist at Bosco. 'My ma is going to kill you and then she's going to divorce you!'

'I should be so lucky.'

Liam whispered to Bosco. 'You're going nowhere till Higs is out of here.'

'You're right I'm going nowhere. I'm staying here tonight again.'

'Well, you'll be the only one here. I'm closing down the bar tonight.'

'But you have another two weeks left.'

'There is practically no stock left and I haven't got the money to buy two more days' worth never mind two more weeks.' Liam was adamant. 'The bar is closing tonight.'

Madge was on her way to the ladies when she overheard Liam. 'What? You're closing the pub tonight. You can't do that! This is my local. I've been coming here since before you were born!'

'Sorry, Madge! The landlord wants to sell it and I don't have the money to buy it. This is your last night in Murphy's Pub.'

'Oh, well, that's fucking great.' Madge stormed off to the toilet, banging the door closed behind her.

Liam looked at his watch. 'I'm closing sharpish tonight. This is our last chance to get Higs back to the chapel.'

Maude, her husband and a small well-rounded man in his sixties arrived at the pub. They took their seats beside Josie.

'How're you Maude, and Peter? Is this the rusty cousin you told Madge about?'

'Josie, this is Willie McQuire,' Maude says. 'Willie is a farmer from Donegal.'

'Oh, a farmer? Have you got cows? I love cows.'

'Indeed, I have, Josie, two hundred of them.'

'Two hundred!' Josie couldn't believe her ears. 'You must have to clean up some amount of shite!'

Madge returned from the ladies and is none too pleased to see Maude sitting there. She pushed her way past, making sure to step on Maude's toes.

'Oh, so sorry!' Madge said sarcastically.

'Madge, look!' Josie was excited. 'Maude was as good as her word. It's yer man, her rusty cousin. His name is… What's your name again, love?'

'I'm Willie.'

'Willie, this is Madge, an old friend.' Maude winked at Madge.

'Less of the old! Hiya, Willie?'

'Well, now,' Willie smiled broadly at Madge. 'I'm very glad to meet you.'

Josie piped up, 'Isn't he a grand man now, Madge? I think that you and him… '

'If you say another word,' Madge said under her breath. 'I'm going to knock you out!'

Bosco went to the toilet seconds before Margie and Cassie come into the pub.

Maureen turned to Connor. 'Oh, dear! My da is about to meet his maker.'

Margie approached Liam with violence in her eyes. 'All right, where is he? And don't bother telling me you don't know. There's not a thing happens in this town that you don't hear about!'

Blissfully unaware of his wife's presence in the pub, Bosco strode out of the gents and straight into the line of fire. When he saw Margie, he tried to slip unnoticed back into the toilet.

'And where do you think you're going?' Margie shouted to his receding back. Bosco stopped abruptly and turned to face his wife.

'Margie, dear, are you looking for me?'

'Don't flatter yourself! Does anyone in here know where Higs is?' The blood drained from Bosco's face. He looked at Liam for help.

Liam stammered,. 'He's in the chapel.'

Margie put her hands on her hips. 'Oh, no, he's not! He's missing and Father Divine won't tell us anything about it.'

Madge choked on her drink. 'Higs is missing! Good riddance, that's what I say. It's a pity he didn't go missing when he was alive and poor Lila wouldn't be sitting in jail tonight!'

'He was meant to get buried today.' Margie looked at her husband. "What's going on?'

'I dunno!' Bosco shook his shoulders.

Margie gave him a scathing look.

'Don't look at me like that. I've been stuck in here helping Liam with stock-taking.'

'And how much stock did you manage to take?' Josie asked. 'I think I'll go over and talk to yer man. Do you know something? He still hasn't said a word. He's the shyest man I ever met.' Josie skipped over to Higs and made herself comfortable beside him. Margie stared at Higs. 'Who's that Josie is talking to? Do I know him?… He looks familiar.'

'No!' Liam said too loudly. 'I mean, you wouldn't know him. He's from Donegal.'

'I don't care where he's from. I'm sure I know him.' She took a few steps towards Higs but Liam came out from behind the bar and blocked her way.

'I know you're not a drinking woman, Margie, but the pub is closing down tonight and I want to offer you and Cassie drinks on the house.'

Madge shouted at the top of her voice, 'You're giving drinks to people who never darken your door and you haven't asked us if we have a mouth on us. You lousy bastard!'

'Drinks on the house for everyone.'

'Now, you're talking.' Madge hurried to the bar. 'I'll have a Southern Comfort, to start. C'mon, Cassie, if you can't beat them, then join them.'

'What's yours, Cassie?'

'I don't drink much, Liam. I'll have a glass of wine, with a whiskey shaker.'

'Coming up.' Liam quickly poured a large round of drinks ordered. 'Right, Bosco, let's hope they all get drunk quickly so we can get them out and get shot of Higs. That man has caused more bother dead than he did alive. I'm going to the storeroom. I think I might have one bottle of whiskey left.' When Liam left the bar, Bosco took the opportunity to pour himself a quick drink.

Margie was still looking at Higs. 'Cassie, don't you think yer man in the wheelchair looks familiar?'

'Sure, he is wearing sunglasses and that blanket is over the bottom half of his face.'

'I know that but, still, something about him is bothering me.'

Bosco took his eyes off his wife for a few seconds and, when he looked up, she is standing beside the wheelchair. Bosco was frozen in horror as she reached for the blanket. Liam came out of the storeroom and saw what was about to happen.

'Margie, no!'

She whipped off the blanket and the sunglasses and Soupy was huddled in the wheelchair in a drunken stupor, fast asleep.

'I could have sworn that he was… '

'Soupy!' Liam laughed hysterically with relief. 'It's Soupy.' He looked at Bosco and mouths the words, 'Where the fuck is Higs!'

Meanwhile, at the bus station, Higs was in the front seat of the Dublin bus. The three drunks stood on the pavement, waving him goodbye. The bus pulled away. As it passed under a street light, the bookie's slip can be clearly seen peeking out of Higs's breast pocket.

THE END

www.ingramcontent.com/pod-product-compliance
Lightning Source LLC
Chambersburg PA
CBHW021720190726
48289CB00008B/2611